GOD, WHY IS SHE THE WAY SHE IS?

DUE

"God, why is she the way she is?"

Written by Linda Jacobs Ware
Illustrated by Michael Hackett

Publishing House
St. Louis

Library of Congress Cataloging in Publication Data

Ware, Linda Jacobs, 1943-
    God, why is she the way she is?

    SUMMARY: An almost-14-year-old who desperately
wants to be grown-up has conflicting emotions about
her mentally handicapped sister.
    [1. Mentally handicapped—Fiction. 2. Brothers
and sisters—Fiction. 3. Christian life—Fiction]
I. Title.
PZ7.W224Go   [Fic]   79-12241
ISBN 0-570-03621-6

Dedication

In memory of Rev. Paul F. Hoy, who encouraged a frightened child to dream—and to Dr. Winthrop Ware, whose love finally made the dreams come true.

Linda Jacobs Ware
Ventura, California
1979

Chapter One

Kelly Marshall tossed on a battered T-shirt and scowled into the mirror. "Pudge. Old Pudge," she muttered to her too-round reflection.

The sound of her mother's voice drifted up the stairway. "Kelly! Becky! Hurry, or you'll be late for the bus."

Kelly shoved her glasses up onto her nose. "Coming, Mom."

She tugged at the ear curls she'd worked so hard to perfect. One was pinned behind the frame of her glasses. The other stuck out from her head like a corkscrew. The hairdo magazine said ear curls were supposed to make "dainty frills against the cheek."

"Some dainty frill," Kelly grumbled. She tugged the corkscrew one last time and went to find her little sister. She heard the hollow sound of water streaming directly into the bathroom drain. Becky. Kelly had become convinced that her little sister knew how to aim that water to get just that sound.

In Kelly's always-active imagination, running water became the sound of applause. The upstairs hallway became the Tres Cerros High School auditorium.

"You've elected Kelly Marshall as freshman class president," someone was yelling into a microphone. Kelly strode onstage, confident and slim after a summer's dieting. "Thank you all for voting for me."

Next fall, that's the way it ought to be. She wanted a class office. Or maybe a part in the school play. Maybe a place on the debating team. Maybe just a first date with a boy. Anything exciting would do. The point was, she had to begin her high school as something besides Klutzy Kelly. She sighed. The applause once again became a water stream hitting directly over the drain.

Becky stood at the bathroom sink, trying to force her toothbrush into the holder bristle-end down.

"Here! This way!" Kelly told her. She sighed and shook her head. Would Becky ever learn? Sometimes she felt like screaming, teaching the same things over and over.

Becky beamed as the handle slid into the holder. Becky beaming was something special. Dimples crinkled into her pink cheeks, and her eyes glowed like brown jewels. Her soft curls—the color of honey with maybe a dash of brown sugar—became a living frame as they bobbled around her face.

"Get taper," she said. Becky scampered into her own room and came out a moment later, holding Kelly's portable cassette recorder. Kelly gave her best you-know-better-than-that look.

"You're not supposed to take that out of my room."

Becky's mouth turned into an upside-down half moon, hanging uncertainly over her chin. "Taper mine someday. You promise."

Kelly grinned in spite of herself. Even with all the problems, it was hard staying mad at this sunny little person. "When you learn to make it go."

Becky patted the plastic case. To her, that machine was all the wonders of the world, rolled into one. When Kelly first bought it, Becky had insisted on recording everyone's voice, especially her own. Then she wanted tapes of everything from the thump-thump of a bouncing ball to the sizzle of bacon frying in the pan.

"I learn," she said. She hugged the recorder close to her chest and bounced downstairs, six steps ahead of Kelly.

"I know you'll learn," Kelly whispered. But it would take a long time. Becky's body was nine years old. Her mind was only about three. Even a simple cassette recorder would be a big deal to a mentally retarded child.

Kelly sighed and shoved her glasses back into place. Mentally retarded. Sometimes she hated the words. She hated having other kids say, "Oh, you know Kelly Marshall—the one with the mentally retarded sister." She hated the way her

8

folks had cried when Becky was born, and the way she had felt guilty, wondering if it was somehow her fault. Kelly scurried down the last steps and grabbed Becky in a big hug, as if to make up for her sad thoughts at the little girl's expense.

"We're on our way, Mom," she called.

Mrs. Marshall came out of the kitchen, dressed in bluejeans and one of her husband's old shirts. At the moment, she smelled like the pine-scented cleaner she used on the floors.

Kelly could usually tell what her mother had been doing by the way she smelled. Spices meant she had been experimenting with another gourmet recipe. The antiseptic scent of the ink from the typewriter ribbon and correction fluid meant that she had been working in Dad's garage, doing the office routines. Motor oil meant she'd been helping with a repair job.

Mrs. Marshall threw a friendly arm around Kelly's shoulder. "Well, this starts your second volunteer summer," she said.

Kelly shrugged and pulled on the brown corkscrew sticking out from the side of her head. "Yeah! Super Teenaide! That's me!"

"Don't make light of it. You're good at your work. And you're dutiful, Kelly."

Kelly grumbled inside and wished her mom was more glamorous, more exciting. "Thanks," she murmured. "See you later."

Good and dutiful—yuck! she thought, as she led Becky out of the house and down the tree-shaded sidewalks of Robles Drive. She would much rather be pretty and popular and be good and dutiful as sort of a sideline.

That was the problem with having been a chubby kid with fat hands, who couldn't even play jacks without missing on her foursies. That was the problem with wearing glasses ever since she was eight; hiding big brown eyes—her only outstanding feature. It made her want to rise above it all, to become the exciting person in her dreams.

As Kelly climbed aboard the blue and white bus, the exciting person hiding inside her acknowledged victory in the student council race. The good and dutiful person jostled along on the belching city bus, taking Becky to summer day camp at the Tres Cerros Academy for Exceptional Children.

The academy—what a lifesaver it had been. The Tres Cerros Association for the Mentally Retarded started it. Kelly remembered that time well; her own parents were on the committee. For weeks the entire Marshall household had hummed with meetings and phone calls, mailings and just-plain-worryings. It was all so small then; but people worked and cared. Parents and older kids donated their time, churches and service clubs helped out. Now there were all kinds of programs for children like Becky; seminars and counseling sessions for the parents, home visits by volunteers—even a free bus for families who couldn't afford transportation.

Kelly sighed as the bus turned the corner. Maybe it wasn't as exciting as winning a student council election, but it had been important to Becky. It always would be. So every summer, old Good-and-Dutiful was there, helping out.

June sunlight bathed the whole seaside town of Tres Cerros in its warmth. The red Spanish tile roofs in Kelly's neighborhood caught fire in its light, and the Pacific whitecaps shimmered into silver.

"Pretty," Becky kept saying. "Pretty."

When they got to the school, the multipurpose room already bustled. Mrs. Riker, the school director, waved a cheery hello. To get across the room she dodged four kids racing toy cars and two more playing house.

"Here we go again," she said to Kelly. Then she turned her full attention to Becky. "We'll have lots of fun this year. We'll go to the beach and the zoo and even to an amusement park."

Becky nodded, but she didn't look at Mrs. Riker. She even ignored the cages that housed her adored Bill and Beulah, the school's pet hamsters.

"They sing," she smiled, pointing to a group clustered around the piano. A Teenaide plunked the notes as the children belted out a loose version of "My Bonny Lies Over the Ocean."

"I taper it," Becky announced and bounced toward the piano like she had springs under her shoes.

Kelly and Mrs. Riker both laughed.

"That Becky's a little ray of sunshine," the director said. Mrs. Riker was fond of corny sayings like that. Sometimes, Kelly thought that was her way to keep from getting discouraged by working with retarded kids.

Mrs. Riker's smile faded. "We've got one coming today who's not a ray of sunshine. Her name is Marcy Simms—most hostile child I've seen in a long time." Mrs. Riker shook her head. Her neatly combed hair hardly swayed. "Her brother Joel—he's a year or so older than you are—will be bringing her. I don't think the parents are much interested."

Kelly gritted her teeth. She knew what was coming. Somewhere along the line she had become the specialist in difficult newcomers. It wasn't fair! There were lots of older Teenaides, kids with more experience. Mrs. Riker patted her arm.

"See to them, will you?"

No, I won't! I've got a lot of exciting plans this summer and I don't want to get tied down doing the same old thing. That's what Kelly thought. All she did was smile and say she'd do all she could. She hated herself for that. Big thoughts. Little acts. Being almost fourteen, she decided, was nothing but a pain. She thought more these days, about being grown-up and exciting. But she was still doing old klutzy-Kelly-kid-things.

"Kelly, come!"

One more dumb thing coming up, Kelly thought. But she went straight to Becky anyway. The little girl was having tape recorder trouble. She'd gotten the microphone into its jack, but she had pushed the "fast forward" instead of the "record" button. Her brown eyes glistened with unshed tears.

"It not go," she wailed.

That was another problem with Becky. She was just smart enough to get impatient with herself. She hated failure—and she got so much of it. Kelly took the machine and quickly pointed out all the things that Becky had done right. The little girl's tears disappeared. Her mouth curved into a half-smile.

Kelly grinned broadly, until her sister showed the dimples in her cheeks. At least Becky could feel better quickly. She never held on to a bad mood for long.

"You'll learn. Don't worry," Kelly said. There was no doubt in her voice. She always held any doubts in firm check. She had learned that half the battle in teaching retarded children was believing that they really could learn—even when that was hard to believe. She patted Becky's arm and then turned to the group.

"Okay. Let's all sing," she said.

The pianist struck a chord. Eager young voices took up the song; "My Bonny lies over the ocean. My Bonny lies over the sea . . ." Those who couldn't manage the words hummed, or simply bellowed. It was an awful sound—rattling and crashing like a tin roof in a rainstorm. Kelly wanted to cover her ears, but she smiled through it all and, when it ended, played back the tape.

Laughter and cries of "I hear me" drowned out the playback. By the time it was over, Kelly's ears were so numb that the voice behind her sounded like an echo in a canyon.

"I'm Joel Simms. Mrs. Riker told me to see you."

Kelly faced a boy with a shock of sandy hair that toppled low onto his forehead. Bright blue eyes glowed beneath brows and lashes so pale they seemed to disappear into his skin. The contrast made him look surprised, even when he wasn't. The most interesting thing about Joel, though, was his hands. The fingers had orange and blue and purple stains all over them.

"I . . . I'm into chemistry," Joel stammered, when he saw Kelly looking at the odd stains.

She smiled. "That sounds interesting," she said. But it didn't sound interesting at all. It sounded dull. "Welcome to our program."

Joel looked like he wanted to run away. He said it was nice to be at the school, but he sounded like he meant about as much as Kelly had meant that chemistry was interesting. He kept glancing down at the little girl beside him. She looked like she was about eight.

"You must be Marcy," Kelly said. "You'll like it here." She reached out and took one of Marcy's hands into her own.

The child scowled. She was a plain kid, with every feature in her face too close to every other feature. It was like the brows and eyes, nose and mouth, had all struggled to fit into a straight line and were frustrated for not quite succeeding.

Joel shifted from one foot to the other. He cleared his throat. "Say hi, Marcy." It sounded almost like a plea.

Marcy didn't speak. She stared silently at Becky, who had come closer to see the new arrival.

Kelly smiled. "Never mind. She's got a right to be shy." This kid didn't look shy though. She looked mad. But Kelly ignored that and told Becky to show the new student around. "Joel and I want to talk," she said.

The two girls were a study in contrasts; sunshine and

shadow. Becky bubbled and bounced, her dimples deeper than usual. She loved showing people through her world. It made her important. "You see paints, doll house, hamsters? I show you!" She skipped ahead, then stopped and turned around. "Come on," she said, not a little sharply.

"Be nice, Becky." That was another problem with Becky. She expected everybody else to get excited when she did. Marcy was not about to live up to that expectation. She planted her feet wide apart and didn't budge. Becky ran back and grabbed her hand. "Come! I show!" she said, pulling the unwilling Marcy along in spite of herself.

Joel's pale eyebrows seemed to want to knit together over the bridge of his nose.

"You be good, Marcy," he called. He sounded more like the voice of doom than someone giving an ordinary warning to a child. His gaze followed Marcy's every move.

Kelly had seen this fear before in new people bringing kids into the program. Relatives tended to get overprotective toward retarded kids. Either that, or they ignored them altogether. Kelly wondered about Joel's interest in Marcy. He didn't seem to like his little sister. A lot of people felt guilty, and they got that all mixed up with love. Joel seemed like one who felt guilty. "Just relax," Kelly said, getting uneasy with the silence. "She'll do just fine."

Joel's eyes, so stark in the pale face, seethed with a mixture of doubt and hope. "I watched you, working at the piano. You really enjoy these kids, huh?"

Kelly flushed and jiggled her glasses. Being watched when she didn't know it always embarrassed her. It was like having somebody read your diary or catch you daydreaming. "Yes, I guess I do." She sighed, hit with a burst of honesty. "At least, sometimes I do."

"And sometimes they can be a pain?"

Kelly nodded and grinned.

"I don't know how you do it; seems to me they'd be a pain all the time. I mean, it takes so much patience. Normal kids, maybe—but these kids?"

Anger snapped inside Kelly, the way it always did when somebody said "these kids" and made it into a putdown. The anger was stronger this time than usual. Today, she was having some of those feelings herself. And she didn't like having them.

"These kids are more normal than they are abnormal. They want love, they want to learn. They want all the things any other kids wants." Kelly had the odd feeling of being a recording, giving the standard speech.

Joel grinned in a sheepish sort of way. "Hey, sorry. I didn't mean to sound like a clod."

"You didn't. It's hard to live with, I know; believe me, I know."

"But you don't admit it very often?"

Kelly felt hot all over, embarrassed, like a child caught swiping cookies. This Joel Simms was no dope. "Not even to myself—when I can help it."

"Thanks for saying it this time. It makes me feel less like a monster. Sometimes, I get so mad at Marcy I could strangle her."

"That's par for the course, I guess," Kelly said, slipping back into her old Teenaide superiority act. But the two smiled at each other, and she knew that they were friends.

"EEEEE" The scream slashed through Kelly's mind. She ran toward the racket, with Joel close behind her. They were the first to burst into an excited group surrounding the hamster cage.

Both of Becky's arms circled Marcy's thin waist. Marcy screamed and wiggled, but Becky planted her feet wide apart and held tight. The other children screamed comments. It was a madhouse. Kelly had to yell for quiet.

"She hurt hamsters," Becky said, when she could finally be heard over the din.

Joel shoved past Kelly and grabbed his sister. One of the hamsters was bleeding and the other cowered in a corner of the cage.

"She poke pencil," Becky cried.

"Marcy! Blast!" Joel looked uncertainly at the quivering little animal. "Will he be okay?"

Kelly reached into the cage and stroked the bleeding little animal. It didn't seem too bad. "I think so."

Joel scooped Marcy up into his arms. "You never do anything right!"

"Don't tell her that!" Kelly said quickly—even though she thought that Joel was probably right about this angry little girl.

"Why not? It's true."

14

"She can learn," Kelly said, but she looked into the pinched little face, so full of hate, and her words sounded stupid to her own ears.

"God, why is she the way she is?" Joel moaned, then stalked away, dragging a squirming and protesting Marcy along in his wake.

Chapter Two

"Will you forget about that guy?" Carol yelled.

Kelly had to pull the phone away from her ear. Dumb. She felt really dumb. That was another problem with being almost fourteen; she felt that way more often these days. Especially around Carol. Cool, pretty Carol—who surely had never felt dumb in her life. She'd called, bubbling with news and wanting Kelly to do her hair. Kelly could only talk about Joel and Marcy. And worry about them.

'Sorry! I guess I can't get with it tonight."

"That's an understatement. You going to call him?"

Kelly sighed, and felt good and dutiful again. "I guess so. Mrs. Riker asked me to."

"Okay. Forget tonight. But don't forget my Fourth of July party."

"I won't," Kelly promised.

How could she forget? Carol's parties were always so grown-up and exciting. In fact, everything Carol did seemed grown-up and exciting. In junior high she had been the first to start acting like a real teenager.

"See you later," Kelly said, and held onto the phone until only the hollow dial tone remained.

"Stupid Joel," she muttered. Lately, being with Carol had become very important. Funny. Kelly had hated her all through elementary school. She remembered fifth grade. She was the fat kid in glasses—the one with the retarded sister. Carol was queen of the May. Tres Cerros Elementary had never given up old-fashioned Mayday celebrations, complete with the streamers on the pole, the flowers in the baskets, and the queen on her crepe-paper covered throne.

Kelly cried when Carol got to be queen. Then and there, she'd made herself a promise. Someday she'd be special, too.

But today wasn't the day. Today was just another time to be super Teenaide. With a sigh, Kelly dialed Joel's number.

He sounded embarrassed at first. Then he grumbled and growled about Marcy, his parents—everything.

"Marcy's been dropped by a couple of schools already— too difficult to handle, they said. Truth is, my folks never helped, just paid their money and ignored the kid. Now she's got to make this summer thing, or Mrs. Riker won't take her in September."

Poor Joel. So that was why he'd gotten so upset. Kelly settled into the little cane chair by the phone stand. "Well yelling at her and threatening to quit is not going to help, you know."

"Do you have to be so merciless?" Joel snapped.

Mrs. Riker had taught Kelly to be direct and honest. No coddling the families. No pity. Lay it on the line.

"I'm only telling you the truth."

There was a long silence. Kelly could hear Joel's breath trembling through the phone.

"You know," he said at last, "the only reason Mom and Dad don't stick Marcy in a state institution is that it would look bad. And they blame me for what happened to her—she got hold of some kerosene or something, when I was supposed to be watching her. So maybe I feel guilty; but anyway, somebody's got to care—do something."

There was a long pause. For once, Kelly didn't know what to say. She remembered her own guilt when Becky was born. Her mother had measles when she was pregnant. Just one of those awful things that happen. Nobody's fault. Yet Kelly managed to blame herself. What would it feel like to have actually made the mistake that cost your kid sister part of her mind?

"Look, I . . . you can't blame yourself. You really can't. Kids get hold of things. . . ," her words tapered off. They didn't seem to mean anything.

"See? Now you know how I feel." Joel sounded almost triumphant. "Look, you're good with these kids. Maybe . . . maybe you could work with Marcy."

Kelly gulped and toyed with her glasses, the way she always did when she was nervous. She felt sorry for Joel. She understood his guilt. But work with Marcy? That would take special sessions. Time. And this wasn't the summer for playing nursemaid to an angry little kid. This was the summer to lose weight and get contact lenses and go to beach parties. This was the summer to start being exciting and sophisticated. A real teenager.

But then there was this skinny little girl nobody loved. Kelly sighed. "We'll have to work extra . . . every day for a couple of hours. And if you think I'm going to do it alone . . ."

"No! Hey, no. I'll help. Thanks! Hey, Kelly . . . thanks a million."

"Sure," Kelly said, and she thought that it ought to be about a billion. "Want to start tomorrow?"

"Yeah! But what do we do? I mean, where do we start?"

The question jumped up like a steel wall, put up just so Kelly could run into it. "I don't know yet. We'll think of something."

She had no idea what that something would be. But two days later, it walked right into their lives. Just in time, too. Kelly had tried talking to Marcy, reading to her—nothing worked. The little girl just tripped off into her own dark world.

Then Joel came in for the morning school session in a huff. He hardly spoke to Kelly. "Com'on, Marcy," he said, "Let's go put you on the swings."

The little girl puckered her face into an angry mask, but she didn't protest. Joel lifted her into a vacant swing next to Becky.

"Hi," Becky called, as she pushed herself higher and higher with quick piston thrusts that raised clouds of dust beneath her feet.

Marcy wrapped her arms firmly around the chains, like she expected to fall any minute. Her thin legs shoved weakly at the ground, moving her in a jerky, rocking motion.

Joel looked from his sister to Becky. Kelly felt she could almost read his mind. "She'll do it. She just needs time to get confidence."

"Yeah, sure!" Joel turned away. He and Kelly moved from the sunlit play yard into the building. His pale eyebrows formed into jagged lines on his forehead.

"Did you ever ask yourself why? Some dumb kerosene—I mean, Marcy was born normal. But some guy who was working for my dad—my dad never does his own work around the house—this turkey left the kerosene out. And I didn't watch. And Marcy—drat—why?"

"There are lots of why's. My mother had german measles in her second month with Becky!"

"That's not *why*," Joel shouted, waving his arms in a wild pattern around his head. "That's how. A disease at the wrong time. A kerosene can in the wrong place. She drank it and—whammo. That's all she wrote. So why?"

Kelly remembered when she and her family had asked that question. She remembered the tears and the late-night visits from the minister and his wife. She remembered the bad dreams about Becky suddenly becoming normal and she, Kelly, turning into a blithering idiot. She remembered feeling guilty because she was glad that—if somebody had to be retarded—it was Becky and not her. That's when she'd wondered if Becky's problem wasn't somehow her fault.

"The only answer I remember," she began slowly, "is that mentally retarded people are human beings with potential. Our job is to accept them as they are and help them find that potential."

Joel's blue eyes grew suddenly icy. "That sounds like a public relations pamphlet for some do-gooder organization. That's not why."

Kelly whirled on him, feeling like she was being pushed in a corner. Then remembering her training, she closed her eyes and took a deep breath. "Joel, I don't have the answer. No one does. Why the black plague in the Middle Ages? Why earthquakes and tidal waves, tornadoes, and car accidents? Why the concentration camps of World War II? I don't know why. You and I are fortunate, Joel. Instead of worrying about the why's, I think you should do something about what is. We should use whatever talents or knowledge we have to help Becky and Marcy . . . that's all I know."

Joel laid his hand on Kelly's arm. She trembled on the brink of tears. "Sorry. Maybe you're right, ask those questions we can answer, like how. You know, I want to be a chemist. Maybe I can use my talent to help one day."

Kelly looked down at Joel's hand on her arm. He pulled it

back like he had touched a hot stove. She smiled and pointed to his stained fingers.

"I can see you like fooling around with chemicals," she said hoping that would put Joel at ease again.

He grinned and a pink glow spread all over his face. "Yeah," he said, waving his hand casually, "I've got a little lab of my own in the garage."

"EEEE . . . Nooo!"

"Marcy!"

Both teenaides scurried outside. Kelly nearly tripped over Billy Jackson, a mongoloid boy who at the moment, was completely preoccupied bewailing a large, bloody scrape on his left knee.

A girl placed Billy's hand into Kelly's.

"Fix him up, would you? That Simms kid pushed him off a swing. She's been a problem ever since you brought her out."

Kelly winced and looked at Joel. He didn't seem to have heard. He was too busy grabbing Marcy.

"I want his swing. His swing go high," the little girl squealed.

"Not his swing," Joel snapped. "The swings are the same. He makes it go high."

"Joel!" Kelly's voice was soft in spite of the warning note in it. "She needs time to learn these things."

Joel seemed to wilt. In two minutes, one antiseptic pad and one small bandage, Billy Jackson was as good as new. Joel Simms wasn't.

"This is all I need. You know, I came in today in a bad mood. . . ."

"I noticed," Kelly cut in. She grinned at him until he could no longer keep from grinning back. Then she turned serious. "What's the problem?"

"Know what my folks got for Marcy? Trying to soften their guilt . . . trying to pretend she's normal, I guess. They got her a puppy. Can you imagine, a puppy—the way she treats living things?"

Kelly had to admit that the idea didn't seem too brilliant. "I hope it's a hardy breed."

"Cockapoo. Marcy will kill the little thing."

Suddenly, an idea flashed through Kelly's mind, clear and exciting. "Maybe not. Maybe we've just found our place to start."

"With the puppy?" Joel smiled, too, catching her excitement.

"Why not? It'll help both Marcy and the puppy."

"Okay," Joel said. "We start with the puppy. Tomorrow?"

Kelly nodded, and in the back of her mind reached out for the private dream that was feeling more shaky every day.

Chapter Three

Kelly was still panting from biking up Seacliff Road when Joel came out to meet her. She barely said hello. She was too busy staring at the stone and wood house that seemed to grow out of the rugged cliffs.

"You live here?" She had never known anyone from the fancy section of town before. "What do your folks do, anyway?" She couldn't resist asking, nor could she hide the awe in her voice.

Joel shrugged. "My mom plays the affluent suburban housewife. My dad is the new president of Coastal Investments." Joel started up the winding driveway and Kelly followed, walking her bike. "What about your folks?"

Kelly wished he hadn't asked that. Not that she was ashamed, but she couldn't help feeling out of her league. "My dad just owns a garage, and my mom helps with the bookkeeping and all that."

"Is your dad a good mechanic?" Joel demanded. He sounded like a gruff Army sergeant, demanding an answer.

"Why—yes—everyone says he has the best service in town."

"How about your mom? Is she a good bookkeeper?" Again, Joel's question turned into a demand.

"Sure she is, she took courses, and—hey, why the third degree?"

"Why do you sound embarrassed when you talk about what they do?" Joel's voice carried a definite snap.

Kelly felt suddenly ashamed of herself. "You're right. It's just that your folks seem so glamorous—anyway, I'm proud of my parents."

Joel didn't say a word. He opened the carved oak door and motioned Kelly inside. "It's a museum, a beautiful museum," he said.

Kelly had to agree with him. The house was a lavender, pink, and purple vision that made her feel like the entire world was created of crushed velvet and lush brocades and mellowed oak. She could imagine invisible DON'T TOUCH signs everywhere. "It's so pretty," she breathed.

"See," Joel said, laughing with a loudness that had to be deliberate, "you're even whispering like you were in a museum."

Kelly blushed and toyed with her glasses so busily that she avoided Joel's challenging gaze. "It doesn't look like a living kind of house," she admitted.

It wasn't a place where people loved and laughed and sometimes cried. No smiling mother greeted her son and his visitor. No warm cookies left a twang of ginger-smell in the air. No books or games or even newspapers were scattered about as unmistakable evidence that the house belonged to a living, breathing family. Kelly would have bet that no tattered slippers lay beside the master bed, the way her father's did at home. She moved through the sterile beauty like the carpet was made of fresh eggs.

Joel grinned. "Come on. My lab is more comfortable."

It was more comfortable. It was also more interesting. Kelly had expected to be bored by the room filled with test tubes and odd-looking bottles and smelling like an anti-pollutionist's nightmare. She hadn't counted on Joel's open enthusiasm and his entirely unexpected knack for explaining complicated experiments in a way that made sense.

"You have a real talent for this stuff," Kelly told him, as they left the lab.

Joel shoved his hair away from its latest skirmish with his eyebrows and grinned. "I guess I do. Like you have a talent for working with retarded kids."

"That's not a talent. It's just something I do. A talent is being able to do something spectacular, like invent things or write books or act in plays, things like that."

Joel shook his head like a minister grieving over the sins of his flock. "That's really a dumb attitude. . . ."

"Hey, thanks!" Before Kelly could think of a good comeback, Joel raised his hands in a gesture of surrender.

"Let's not fight. Marcy will be in the housekeeper's cottage."

Kelly followed Joel across the back yard. It had a "don't touch" sign, just like the house. Gardenia bushes grew next to the wood fence, and a rose garden occupied a center circle in the velvety lawn. The smells blended in such sweetness that Kelly thought she could close her eyes and move to some lush, tropical paradise.

Joel led her to a stone cottage that looked like something out of a fairy tale. "There's an old stable just up the path," he said, pointing to a winding cobblestone walkway that led to a gate in the fence. "We can work there."

Kelly nodded and then waited on the path until Joel brought Marcy and a small brown dog from the cottage. Both the dog and the child looked out of place in that gardener's paradise.

They didn't look out of place in the field by the stable. It was filled with crabgrass and dandelions that could stand the trampling of childish feet.

The puppy scampered about, dancing in front of them. His pink tongue tried to make contact with everything in reach. Kelly knelt down to pet him. "He looks like an animated mop," she laughed, as the shaggy mass of wriggling warmth cast itself into her arms. "Does he have a name?" she asked Marcy.

The little girl stared into the open sky and shook her head, as if answering some far-off question that had nothing to do with Kelly.

Joel scowled at her. "Only thing I could think of for a Cockapoo was Rags," he said, "but that's not too original."

"I guess not." Kelly rocked her glasses up and down on her nose. Somehow that helped her think. "How about Tatters?" she blurted, giving the glasses a final push.

Joel didn't say anything, but his eyes sparkled.

The puppy's name was Tatters.

"How does that sound to you two?" Kelly asked, as she held the squirming puppy out to Marcy.

The puppy wagged his tail and licked the air in the general direction of Marcy's face. Marcy's beak of a nose twitched, and her features arranged themselves into a scowl. She stood still for a moment, then reached for the newly named Tatters. Her thin hands wrapped around the small body like the talons of an eagle, tearing into a rabbit.

25

"Ki'yi'ki'yi," ripped through the summer air.

Joel jerked the puppy free. He clutched the trembling little animal close to him. His whole face drooped like a wilting plant. "Looks like poor Tatters is going to be tattered in more ways than one."

Kelly reached out one hand to Marcy and the other to the puppy.

"Gentle . . . gentle." She stroked Marcy's arm and Tatter's back with the same firm, repetitive motion. She looked up at Joel and smiled in what she hoped was a reassuring way. "It takes patience. And there'll be setbacks. Those are the rules of the game."

Joel seemed to understand. He muttered something about being sure the puppy didn't get hurt. Then he got back to work. He was awkward with Marcy and the puppy, always asking Kelly what to do, how to act.

"Act natural. Show her," Kelly would say.

Joel tried. Over the next few days, he began to loosen up. He seemed almost happy with the work. Then Marcy managed to sneak the puppy into the house one morning when Mrs. Simms was at one of her club meetings. When Kelly came to the house that day, everything was in turmoil."

"Tatters wet the floor," Joel grumbled, "and mom spanked him. Now Marcy spanks the poor little thing every five minutes." He pushed the hair away from his forehead and flopped onto the ground next to the weathered stable. "All my mother knows about being a mother is how to look good at PTA meetings." At that moment, Joel looked like he wanted to resign from life. "How did I get into this in the first place?"

"Because you care."

"Because I feel guilty, you mean. And why should I? I mean, I didn't let her get hold of the kerosene on purpose, did I? Anyway, what's the use? She'll never do anything important. God, why is she the way she is?"

"Wait a minute," Kelly yelled, her voice cracking with the rush of anger. "She is what she is—a human being. She counts. Anyway, aren't you always the one who puts me down for wanting to be special—*to count*?"

Joel didn't say another word.

He stuck with the project and worked hard. On July third, Marcy made her first progress. Joel nearly danced through the crabgrass.

"She played with Tatters for ten minutes . . . like a normal kid . . . never once hurt him." Joel picked a wilting dandelion and held it up like a victorious warrior raising his sword. "I hereby declare this Fourth of July my personal Independence Day!"

Kelly laughed and shook her head. "Remember now, this is just a first step. She still needs . . ."

"Spoil sport! Don't talk setbacks now. Let's celebrate. There's an outdoor concert tomorrow night . . . . I read about it in the paper. Maybe we can go." He gulped and turned pink around the ears, like he just realized he had asked a girl for a date. "How about it? We—I mean, we deserve some fun."

"It sounds great. I think . . ." Kelly broke off, remembering. "Oh-h-h, I promised my girl friend I'd come to her party. Want to come? It would be great. Carol was the most popular girl in our junior high! Of course, it'll be mostly freshmen, I guess, but . . ."

"I don't care about that . . . I mean, it being freshmen. But I hate parties. I'll pass."

"But you could meet everybody."

"I don't *want* to meet everybody."

Kelly didn't know how to answer. So she said nothing. Good old antisocial Joel. He'd probably stay home and get more chemical stains on his fingers. She figured he wouldn't go to the concert by himself. Joel didn't like being social, but then he didn't like doing things alone, either. He was a one-friend type of guy.

Well let him be, Kelly thought. She was going to be social and popular, have lots of friends. She would go to the party. And she would have fun.

"Maybe we can go to another concert."

"Maybe!" Joel sounded sulky.

Kelly put the whole thing out of her mind and went home. But that night, when she picked over her closet to choose the perfect party dress, she thought about Joel and the concert. She decided to wear the yellow cotton with the tiny flowers and long, full skirt. It looked good. Kind of soft and romantic and perfect for an exciting party. It even made her look skinnier than she really was.

She pictured a slim Kelly, without glasses, laughing and talking with the most popular kids in the incoming freshman class. Carol would be jealous because Old-Klutzy-Kelly stole the show at *her* party. Boys would pay attention, and nobody—but nobody—would remember that she was the one with the retarded sister.

That, Kelly decided, was surely better than going to some dull old concert with a stick-in-the-mud like Joel. "But why," Kelly asked her image in the mirror, "do I halfway wish I was going to that dumb ol' concert?"

Chapter Four

Kelly didn't feel skinnier in the dress, her corkscrew curls wouldn't cork, and the glasses sat on her nose like usual. It wasn't exactly the best beginning for a great evening. Neither was Carol's greeting when she got to the door.

"A dress? Didn't I tell you this was a fem lib party?"

Carol's laughter chimed like ice cubes on crystal glasses. Kelly could have throttled her. "No, you didn't," she said, and couldn't help wondering if Carol had "forgotten" on purpose. That was too mean to think about seriously, though. So Kelly smiled and laughed and wished she had gone to that dumb concert with Joel. She also wished she had worn pants.

"I'm so liberated," she said, "that I don't have to wear pants to prove I'm liberated."

Carol laughed again and made an invisible mark in the air—her sign for "your point." Then she drifted away and Kelly stood alone just inside the doorway.

Rock music throbbed in her ears. Bright wall posters glared slogans: WOMEN ARE PEOPLE . . . DOWN WITH MALE CHAUVINISTS . . . INDEPENDENCE DAY FOR WOMEN. The place smelled of onion, cheese, and hot bean dip.

Across the room, Kelly spotted Brian Greer. Just like Carol, she thought with a quick burst of anger. She'd have to invite somebody as a status symbol. Who better than Brian Greer? He was fifteen already and big for his age, with the golden tan and trim muscles that—in another couple of years—would be perfect if surfer movies ever came back.

Carol had said a long time ago that she wanted Brian Greer for her first real boyfriend. So she was starting already. Figured. Some girls just always managed to be Mayday Queen.

Kelly sighed and wandered to the refreshment table. She dunked a corn chip into spicy brown beans and thought of her diet just as she ate it. Tomorrow, she told herself, and tried the onion dip. Dumb Carol. Why was she in such a big hurry to grow up, anyway? Carol was the only girl Kelly knew who had been happy when her periods started. Her big thing in life was getting to wear a bra so she could burn it. Big deal, Kelly thought. Real fem lib. Kelly made a face and grabbed a handful of peanuts.

If Carol was going to be Miss Sophisticate—with Brian Greer—then *she* needed comfort. And food was as comforting as anything she could think of at the moment.

She ate too much of it, though, and drank too much pop. Then she polished everything off with a gorgeous banana split that made her feel thoroughly ashamed of herself. She hardly talked to anybody, and she was downright glad when Carol's mom said it was time for everybody to go home.

Kelly walked alone into the velvet night, listening to the other kids' laughter mingle with cricket songs. She told herself that it really was, after all, a wonderful party. It was bright and fun and kids she'd known all her life had seemed like grown-up strangers. She had been part of it all, too. Nothing could take that away. Even stuffing her face and feeling lonely—she had been part of it.

The next day Kelly told Joel about the wonderful party and found that the telling brought even more believing. He never seemed to notice that her most detailed descriptions were of the food. Kelly hardly noticed that herself.

"I'm glad you had fun," Joel said, leaning back on the stump of a California Oak and watching Marcy play peacefully with Tatters. Kelly was put out that Joel didn't volunteer any information about the concert, but she checked her curiosity.

"Yeah." Kelly jiggled her glasses and looked for a way to change the subject. "Marcy's doing great."

Joel nodded and his pale eyebrows drew closer together. "In a way. But she's still wild . . ." when Kelly started to cut in, he held up his hand. "I know. I know. It takes time."

Kelly just nodded. Joel plucked a blade of grass and gnawed on the juicy end. "Do you really like parties?" he blurted.

"Sure. Who doesn't?"

"*I* don't!"

"I shouldn't have asked." Kelly flopped forward onto her stomach, puckering her mouth into such a disgusted look that they both started laughing. Then they fell into a pointed silence. Questions, unasked, zipped around between them. Kelly could tell from the way that Joel squirmed, he was as uncomfortable as she was.

As she watched Marcy, Kelly's thoughts turned to her own little sister and to the difference between the two girls. She wished that Joel's parents had showed more concern for Marcy, instead of having treated her like a curse inflicted upon the family. She could hardly be too angry with them, though. Having a mentally retarded child in the family wasn't easy; it hadn't been with Becky. More than once Kelly had found her mother with tears in the corner of her eyes.

Kelly remembered asking her mother the same question Joel blurted out the day Marcy pushed Billy Jackson from the swing: "Mom," she had said, "why is Becky the way she is? Is God punishing us?"

"God doesn't punish innocent children, Kelly," her mother had replied. "He loves Becky just as we should love her. She is God's special gift to us. It's our opportunity to show love for Him."

Love, Kelly thought, was something Marcy needed to understand and feel, and perhaps Tatters could help her grasp a sense of that emotion.

Suddenly Kelly remembered she had forgotten to tell Joel the big news.

"I finally talked my folks into getting me contact lenses; next week, I go in."

To Kelly, that was big news. She'd begged for a year and finally, this morning at breakfast, her father had read a news article about soft lenses. They sounded safe enough, he said. He and her mother winked at each other a lot, then asked Kelly if she would like to make an appointment with Dr. Clark. Would she? She could hardly wait.

Joel didn't sound as impressed as she felt. He just grumbled silently, then shrugged. "I don't know why anybody would go around sticking pieces of plastic in their eyes."

"Why would anybody put on a stupid metal harness filled with coke bottle bottoms?"

"To see!"

Kelly rolled onto her back and grinned up at the pale boy. "What do you think contacts are for? Eating?"

"Oh, never mind."

They both laughed, and then were silent. This time, the silence didn't seem so awkward. It was comfortable and friendly. Friendly—yuck! Kelly had thought maybe—just maybe—she and Joel might be more than friends. He was no Brian Greer, but at least he was a boy. It wasn't going to happen, though. Joel wasn't ready. He was too busy getting his fingers stained. And, Kelly guessed with a sigh, she wasn't ready, either. She'd never admit that to Carol, though.

Kelly pushed her thoughts into the back of her mind, tucked neatly into the same corner where she kept storing her diet and her unformed plans for fame and fortune.

The one plan that did come out of that corner was her contact lenses. She got them on the day before the center's beach party. They were plastic circles that she could fold in her fingers. Dr. Clark hadn't been sure about fitting a girl so young, but Mrs. Marshall had gone on about how mature Kelly was; how well she took care of her things.

Old good and dutiful again, Kelly thought, but at least this time it paid off.

The lenses didn't hurt—exactly. But Kelly's eyes teared a lot and her nose ran. Dr. Clark said that would pass in a few days. Good, Kelly thought. But that didn't stop her from being nervous, or from using a whole box of tissues. It didn't stop her from almost deciding to wear her glasses on beach day.

"No," she told herself, and dutifully popped her lenses into her eyes. She sniffled and blinked hard.

She was still sniffling as she climbed aboard the ancient yellow bus that served as the school's only means of transportation.

Laughing children and their supervisors crammed the seats while towels and balls, brightly colored pails, shovels, and innumerable picnic baskets spilled into the aisle.

In the midst of all the confusion, Marcy had insisted on bringing Tatters.

"She wouldn't leave him home," Joel grumbled for the third time that morning.

"I keep telling you it means she's getting attached," Kelly said. She looked around at grinning children who stretched across the aisle and stumbled over picnic baskets to pet a little brown dog. Becky was so thrilled with Tatters that she never once checked Kelly's lap for that ever-present "taper."

"Anyway," Kelly added, "all the kids are enjoying

Tatters. He adds to the fun." She sniffed and dug into her denim purse for a tissue.

Joel grinned at her. "Those things bothering you?"

"A little, but not for long."

He turned a sudden bright red. "Well, I gotta admit, they do make you look nice." He looked away from Kelly's answering smile and quickly changed the subject. "What do you want to bet we'll be stuck taking care of Tatters at the beach?"

Kelly hardly heard him. She was too busy glowing over her first contact lens compliment. Sure, it wasn't exactly like she dreamed it. Some regular Brian Greer type would come up to her and say, "Wow, you're really pretty without those glasses." It wasn't quite that glamorous. But it was something. "What did you say?" she asked, pulling herself out of the dream.

She laughed when he patiently repeated himself. "Don't be so glum. It could be worse. Suppose somebody decided to bring Bill and Beulah along?"

Joel sputtered like a dying auto engine. "That's all I need—hamster-sitting!"

They both laughed as the bus jostled and jounced its way down a road that wound past two drive-in restaurants, a palm-shaded motel, and a diving supply store. The bus turned into the concrete parking lot that stretched to touch the sun-brightened sand. It belched to a halt, and the doors creaked open.

Everybody and everything spilled out the door. The group with all its equipment resembled a small invasion force, spreading over the warm sand.

Laughing children splashed at the edge of the water, scooped wet sand into eager hands, and chased beach balls. A couple of the kids made sand castles that perhaps weren't as fancy as other kids' work, but they were cried over just as much when the water washed them away.

Tatters sat on an old pink blanket with Kelly and Joel.

"Didn't I tell you?" Joel said, his voice as dry as a desert breeze invading the moist, salt-tinged air.

Kelly laughed and patted the puppy. "Look at it this way . . . maybe Tatters needs a suntan." She rubbed her eyes and blew her nose. "Wish I'd brought sunglasses."

"That's brilliant. Get contact lenses and then have to wear

sunglasses all the time."

So much for her first compliment, Kelly thought. She hated Joel for wrecking it.

"Will you just shut up?"

He made a face at her and flopped onto his stomach. They had one of those comfortable-friend silences they'd been falling into lately. Kelly turned over, too, letting the sun's bright warmth caress her back. She blew her nose again—with a side glance at Joel—and then watched the children romp; their happy shouts blending with the rumble of ocean waves.

She laughed, sharing a sense of discovery, when a tall black girl let Becky hold a conch shell. The little girl ran her hands over the rough surface. Her eyebrows drew together, and her mouth puckered as she turned it around and around in her hands. Finally, she sniffed at it and then licked it three times. When neither touch nor smell nor taste could tell her anything, she held the conch to her ear.

Becky screeched. The shell flipped out of her hand like it was propelled by some unseen force. She backed away from it—and her startled new friend—to run to Kelly as fast as her chubby legs would churn through the sand.

"Something there, Kelly," she said, bouncing the words like they were so many rubber balls.

Both Joel and Tatters startled at the fear in Becky's voice. The child picked up the little dog and cuddled him as if he was the last thing standing between her and utter disaster.

"Something there, Kelly," she repeated, her eyes wide.

The tall girl had come up to the little scene, looking almost as frightened as Becky. "I'm sorry. I bought it at the shell shop—thought she'd like it."

"Don't worry," Kelly said gently. "May I use it for a while?"

The girl nodded. Kelly wrapped a comforting arm around her little sister. Becky leaned against her and let Tatters scamper to the ground.

"It's just a sound, only a sound," Kelly told her. She held out the shell, making no move to force Becky to take it. She put it to her own ear. "See? Only a sound, like the ocean."

Kelly offered her free hand to Becky and led the child right to the water's edge. "Listen!" she said, and the sense of wonder in her voice softened the command to gentleness. She slowly

35

moved the shell to Becky's ear. "Listen!" she said again.

Becky's whole face formed into circles of wonder that rounded her eyes and mouth, plumped her cheeks. Then her eyebrows and her lips puckered with the force of some new idea. She pulled back from the shell like it was a live bomb.

"Water in there? Big water . . . get wet, Kelly."

Kelly always tried hard not to laugh at her sister's misunderstandings. But she couldn't help a gentle chuckle at this one. "No . . . only a sound," she said, and then paused, casting about in her mind for a way to explain the difference between sounding like the ocean and having its true powers.

"Like on the taper," she said at last, seizing on the best explanation available. "Go get me the taper, I'll show you."

Becky scampered to the blanket and back in what seemed like two leaps.

Kelly first held the microphone toward the sea, then played back its roaring rumble, safely captured on the innocent "taper." Then she held the microphone all the way inside the conch shell and played back the gentler rumble.

Becky listened to the two sounds again. She shut off the recorder and stared at the ocean. For a moment, her face was like a blackboard wiped clean. Then her eyes widened and her mouth spread into a dimpled smile.

"Sound," she laughed, reaching for the conch. The way she gripped it to her, Kelly knew that the evil thing had become a friend.

"Give it back to the lady now."

Becky held out the shell. The black girl smiled and then shook her head, looking at Kelly. "You did that great," she said, and then left, with a friendly wave.

Kelly went back to the blanket and plopped down beside Joel. "Let's hope this is the last crisis of the day," she said, and blew her nose for what seemed like the hundredth time.

Joel shook his head. His mouth twisted up at one corner as he made a sound that was half sigh, half grunt. "Who else could have handled that so well?" he asked. "Now will you listen to me when I say that working with these kids takes talent?"

"Nope," Kelly said, and grinned.

"Okay. Okay. We'll just settle for hoping this is the last crisis of the day."

It wasn't the last crisis.

Billy Jackson stepped on a jagged piece of glass. Janie Turner popped a beach ball and cried like she'd lost the crown jewels. Everybody dropped food into the sand, choked on it, or simply ate too much of it.

Kelly figured that both Marcy and Tatters would need big doses of Pepto Bismol by the end of the outing. Marcy stuck a skinny hand into the picnic basket at least twelve times that day. Each time, she pulled out a new treat. Each time, she gave Tatters part of the goody.

Kelly knew she ought to stop it. And she almost did. But when the little girl pulled out a cupcake and did a teasing dance in front of Tatters, she didn't have the heart to break it up.

She nudged Joel to watch as Marcy skipped toward the water. It was the first time either one of them had seen her skip. She usually plodded flatfooted, in her mad-at-the-world way. Tatters scampered at her side, leaping to catch the crumbs she threw for him.

"See?" Kelly said happily, "She's actually having fun with him. They'll both be chocolate from end to end, but . . . MARCY!"

The little girl suddenly scooped up the wriggling puppy, ran into the ocean, and heaved him far out into the frothing waves.

Joel shot for the water, with Kelly close behind. Tatter's yelps had already turned to gurgles when Joel reached him. A group of children and staff gathered to watch Joel bring forth a soggy, whining bundle of sheer misery.

"He can't swim. I thought all dogs could swim," he said.

Joel handed the puppy to Kelly. Someone else gave her a towel. Tatters trembled in Kelly's arms like he had a vibrator in his small body. Kelly wrapped him in the warm, dry cloth and began toweling him off.

"He all right?" "Puppy okay?" "Not dead?"

Children popped questions from all around her. Becky stood beside her sister, reaching out to pat Tatters gently on the head.

"He's all right," Kelly said, cuddling the little animal close.

Joel glared at Marcy. The flush in his face had nothing to do with the day's suntan. "I thought she was doing so great." The words seemed to stick in his throat.

"Remember the setbacks," Kelly said, her voice soft beneath the sniffle she couldn't control. She held out the puppy to Joel. "Here. He's okay."

Joel was shaking. "No. You keep him, Becky will be good to him, and . . . well, thanks for trying." He grabbed Marcy's hand. "Come on," he said, jerking his silent but scowling sister along beside him.

"Where are you going? It's not time to leave . . . the bus . . ."

"I'll take a city bus," Joel cut in, "or I'll walk. I've had it, Kelly. I've just had it. I'm through worrying, through feeling guilty—through trying."

Kelly followed him, her feet slipping in the loose sand. "Now, look. You don't mean that . . ."

Joel kept walking.

In desperation, Kelly grabbed his arm, pulling with such force that he turned in the sand. "Now you just wait! Who promised easy? It's not easy, Joel. It's hard. It's working step by step and not knowing when or if you're going to get through. But it's believing you will . . . somehow. And all of it counts . . . the patience and the work . . . it counts because people count. You're always asking God, why is she the way she is. Why don't you forget that and ask God for strength to do what *you* can to help?"

Joel whistled softly under his breath. His face reddened slowly, making his pale eyebrows disappear even more into his forehead. "Do you really believe that, I mean . . ."

"Everybody counts . . . or nobody. That's what my folks said when they got through feeling sorry for themselves about Becky. How do you draw the line? Who's going to decide what kind of people aren't worth worrying about? That's what my dad said; he's pretty philosophical for a mechanic, I guess. But believing it has kept us going."

"How do you do it?" Joel's voice shook on the edge of tears that Kelly knew he would be embarrassed to shed.

"Just keep believing, I guess." Kelly smiled softly at her friend. "Try. Trying makes it easier to accept . . . or at least easier to live with."

Joel didn't answer right away. Kelly stared silently at him. Her contact lenses itched, her nose was ready to run again, and every nerve in her body screamed.

At last, Joel relaxed.

"Okay. Back to it tomorrow?"

Kelly nodded and breathed a sigh of relief.

Chapter Five

Kelly lay flopped on her bed, trying to read a copy of *Seventeen*. She thought about Joel and the close skirmish at the beach. Since then, things hadn't seemed right. Kind of low-key. Blast Joel anyway, asking all those questions that even the wisest people couldn't answer. What good was a retarded person's life? What good was anybody's life?

She sighed and told herself to keep believing. That's all she could do, keep believing. And try to be something special.

Outside, rain pelted her window, and the sky looked like grey mud. It was one of those summer rains that always seemed to come just at the wrong time.

It made Kelly feel at loose ends. She still hadn't thought of anything new to try with Marcy. She had started her diet and only lost two pounds after days of torturing herself by eating carrot sticks and dreaming of double malteds or hot dogs with the works. Then there was the matter of the contact lenses. She was used to them now. The sniffling had stopped. She hardly felt them in her eyes.

But no doors had opened. Nobody gave a party in her honor or begged her to run for student council next fall. The only compliment she'd gotten was Joel's, that day at the beach. And he probably just said it because he knew that's what she wanted to hear. Kelly laughed at herself, though the laughter never quite made it to the level of sound. It was stupid. She felt lousy when she didn't get compliments. Then when she did get them, she felt lousy because they probably weren't sincere. That, she decided, must be another problem that went along with being almost fourteen.

It had to change. It just had to. That night, with the copy of *Seventeen* in her lap, Kelly took a vow. She would stick to that diet. No more excuses. And she would run for a freshman class office.

She didn't know how to start on her newly born political career. But she knew how to find out. Caught in her new determination, she pulled her yellow terrycloth robe closer about her and padded barefooted to the hallway phone. She dialed Carol's number from long memory. Her friend sounded breathless when she answered.

"I'm getting ready for a wiener roast. Brian's going to be there . . . a bunch of older kids."

"And your folks will let you go?"

"Sure. You know how my dad wants me to be in with the best people."

"Yeah," Kelly said, and sighed. Good old Carol—always getting everything, and having folks who helped. "Hey, reason I called, I'm thinking about running for student council next fall."

Carol cooed and giggled a bit and said that was a great idea. "You need something besides working with those kids."

Kelly didn't like the way she said "those kids," but in Carol's case, she passed it over. Nobody would dare call Carol down for anything. "Got any ideas on how to start?

"Sure!" Carol had ideas about everything. "They're holding the elections at freshman orientation, before school starts. It's new this year." Carol talked in that excited but crisp voice she used when she was presenting herself as the final authority on everything of importance. In a rush of words, she told Kelly about the election rules and about the new office of Freshman Class Advocate. "It's perfect for you. You poll the kids about what they want, handle gripes, report to the student council." Carol trailed off, her quick enthusiasm spent. "Just don't run for secretary," she said, "that's what I'm going to be."

That was like Carol. She just took it for granted that she'd win whatever office she wanted. Kelly made a face into the phone. Carol's confidence was no easier to take because it was right. She would win. She would be Freshmen Class Secretary, just like she had been Mayday Queen.

It wasn't fair. Carol's folks spent money on her all the time—clothes, dancing lessons, music lessons, even modeling school. Carol was their only child—there was no retarded sister to eat up the family income with special education needs.

Kelly felt mean for her sudden flash of annoyance at Becky, just because she existed. Since her little sister wasn't around to receive some extra guilt-attention, she was extra nice to Carol.

"You're really great for helping me," she said.

"Uh-huh!" Carol's mind had obviously turned back to the wiener roast. "Hey, I'll see you later, okay?"

"Okay." Kelly hung up, feeling like a two-year-old abandoned on the freeway.

It would be a big job to make her dream come true. A big, scary job. For days, Kelly had half her mind on it no matter what she was doing. She thought about it when she saw the sophisticated girls in *Seventeen*. She thought about it every time she was hungry because of the stupid diet. It was like some kind of ghost living inside her.

She didn't manage to put it aside until the day of the school's zoo trip. That was too hectic for thinking. She could only do. Get everyone on the bus and into their seats. Keep them quiet while the old buggy chugged down the freeway toward Los Angeles. Wipe noses. Break up fights. Tell a sweating child for the fiftieth time that she couldn't help how hot it was.

"Oh, murder," Kelly whispered, as she sank back into her seat for what seemed like the hundredth time.

Joel laughed and winked at her. "Don't tell me the great Kelly Marshall is running out of patience?"

Kelly wrinkled her nose at him. "I'm not out of patience. I'm a saint, haven't you heard? I'm just ready to kill them, that's all."

Laughter died in Joel's eyes. "Did you ever think of that for real? That they'd be better off dead, I mean . . ."

More of those stupid unanswerable questions that only made her feel bad! Kelly started to answer a quick and self-righteous NO. But that would be a lie. "Sometimes, with the more severe ones," she stammered.

"I'm glad . . . I mean, it makes me feel more human, knowing you've at least thought that way. I did, about Marcy, especially when I believed it was all my fault, the way she is.

42

Then I thought God was punishing me for not watching her right."

"Do you really think God would do that? The trouble with you, Joel, is that you don't have faith in yourself, in your parents . . . or even in God."

"You must have thought about this a lot," Joel said softly.

"I did."

Squeals from the children silenced the talk as the bus pulled into the zoo parking lot. The whole park spread out before them like a fairy land, laced with paths that led to Africa or South America or the Arctic. Each child found something special that seemed meant just for him.

Becky thrilled to birds with bright feathers. She taped the sounds of the aviary with only help in pushing the record button at the proper time. Marcy liked the timber wolves. Kelly and Joel had to do some fancy explaining to keep her from climbing the fence and "petting puppies."

"How do you convince a kid that timber wolves aren't exactly harmless puppies?" Joel laughed. He seemed more relaxed, more accepting of Marcy than ever before.

"I don't know, but let's hope one of them isn't named Tatters, or we're really in trouble."

Marcy was willing enough to leave the wolves and follow the group to new and just-as-exciting places. Still, the hippos that made Janie laugh and the lions that Charlie liked only made her reaffirm how much better she liked the "puppies."

Even Billy Jackson's favorite giraffes weren't anything compared to those big puppies.

"Ugh!" Marcy said of the gangly creatures.

Billy obviously didn't agree. "Up! Up! Up!" he muttered as his gaze traveled the length of a seemingly endless neck. When at last his line of sight had reached the giraffe's head, Billy was so off-balance that he toppled to the ground.

All the children laughed, even Billy, who was usually self-conscious about his defective balance. It was just not the kind of day for self-consciousness or tears or any unhappy thing.

It was a day for enjoying the smell of cotton candy, for feeling good just because the cool breeze dried the sweat on your upturned face.

It was a day for spending half an hour watching the antics of the chimpanzees. The animals played with one another like mischevious children on the first day of summer vacation. They took turns carrying one another "piggy back," did good imitations of rock and roll dancing, and generally did everything in their power to convince visitors to disobey signs that said, in big red letters DO NOT FEED THE ANIMALS.

One big male came to the edge of the ditch that separated the chimp area from the fence above it. He chattered and bounced until he had the full attention of the crowd. When everybody watched only him, the chimp pulled on both corners of his mouth and folded his lips back so that the pink skin underneath made a wide gash in his dark face.

Everybody laughed.

The chimp earned his peanuts, and the people who fed him earned a warning from the park guard.

The chimps didn't take long to notice that the guard had cut their food supply. They gave up the show and went back into their caves.

The group moved on, to the children's zoo. It was a special section, set aside from the rest of the huge park. Small humans and small animals could get to know each other in the most basic way of all—by touch.

Marcy wandered in a daze, inspecting every animal, running her fingers over them with movements as hungry as a blind person's.

Becky ignored everything but a lamb she stroked, cooing softly. Her face had the same innocence as the baby animal's. She beamed with excitement, softened to tenderness.

Every other child found a special animal. The fact that these creatures could be touched and fondled made them instant favorites over all the full-grown hippos and elephants and giraffes that had been seen only from a distance.

EEEEEEEEEE! The piercing squeal of a hurt animal slashed through the complex. Joel and Kelly looked around for Marcy.

They found her with one of the zoo attendants who had just grabbed a baby rabbit from her.

"She was jerking his legs," the attendant snapped. He held the rabbit the way Joel and Kelly had so often held Tatters.

Joel mumbled some kind of an apology and led Marcy outside.

"Go back,"she wailed, pulling against him.

45

Joel shook her—hard. Marcy started screaming, fat tears rolling down her thin face. "God, why is she . . .?"

"Stop it!" Kelly said. Her voice was sharp, no nonsense. "Remember the setbacks," she said, more gently. She knelt next to Marcy. "All animals have feelings—like Tatters."

Marcy cocked her head to one side, listening with the strained expression of someone trying to pick out a few words from a foreign language.

At least she was listening, trying to understand. For the first time, she seemed to want to learn. That, Kelly knew, was half the battle.

"Joel, you work and work, trying to teach a child something—and then you somehow get a clue about where to go next. Mrs. Riker says it's like finding a key to a locked mind."

Kelly scooped Marcy into her arms. "We're going to get all kinds of animals . . . and show you how to treat all of them."

Marcy stared without understanding, but Joel's blazing anger flashed into joy. "Hey—you think it will really work?"

Of course, I think it will work, why else would I try it, Kelly thought. But she didn't say that. It wouldn't be fair. She was still annoyed with Joel for the way he shook Marcy. She'd have to talk to him about that—later. He ought to realize that it was pretty dumb, trying to teach a child to be gentle by being rough with her.

"Let's borrow some animals and start finding out."

Chapter Six

The big roundup started the next day. By evening Kelly and Joel rescued a flop-eared mutt and an orange cat from the pound and bought an adult white rabbit. They even promised a family going on vacation that they would take care of the family's Shetland pony. He was chocolate brown, with a billowing, cream-colored mane and tail.

The weathered stable in the crabgrass field teamed with life.

"Imagine this . . ." Joel gestured toward the animals, "in an executive-level family." He put on a look of mock horror, as Kelly imagined his folks might have done. Then he grinned and slapped his hands onto his hips. He leaned back like a rancher surveying his spread.

Kelly giggled. "It could ruin your mother's image."

"Yeah," Joel said, and his sly smile made Kelly giggle even more.

"Your mother's not one of your favorite people," she said, turning suddenly serious.

"That's okay," Joel said, "she's one of *her* favorites."

"Ouch."

Joel shrugged. "I love her, really. I mean . . . she's my mother and all. I don't even mind all her social games." He clenched and unclenched his stained fingers. "You know what I really don't like? The way she tries to ignore Marcy's problem . . . I mean, when she isn't trying to blame me for it. Sometimes she acts like retardation doesn't exist and sometimes, like Marcy doesn't."

"Mrs. Riker says lots of people try to dodge the truth."

"Yeah, well, my mom's sure doing a good job there." Joel shoved both his hands into the pockets of his jeans. "You think it's terrible, don't you? I mean, not liking my own mother . . ."

"Not really! I guess you can love somebody without liking them."

"Yeah . . . now that's how I feel." Joel grinned at Kelly in silent thanks for her understanding. "Come on, let's get to work."

They started with the Shetland Pony.

"His name is Ranger," Kelly told Marcy.

The little girl wound her fingers into the thick cream mane. She didn't speak, but a wordless gurgle made it plain that Ranger had to be the most interesting animal in the world.

Joel's pale face creased into a wide grin. "It's looking good, I got to admit, it's looking good."

Marcy played with Ranger for an hour. She nuzzled her face against his, told Joel again and again to put her on his back. Then she would slide off, smiling to herself.

That hint of a smile on the pinched little face was a miracle to Kelly. Marcy was still off in her own little world most of the time. She was still angry and suspicious a lot. But she was changing.

Kelly felt so good about that first session with Ranger that the bike ride home was pure joy. The ocean breeze slapped at her face and left the smell of salt in her nose. Houses and trees and flower gardens whizzed past. Kelly usually was out of breath when she rode this fast. But she'd already lost eight pounds. She could ride easier now, zipping along and letting herself dream about the wonderful new Kelly Marshall, who would be romantic and grown-up. And it was all happening. In spite of the time she spent at the program and with Marcy, she was doing something about the dream. At that moment the world seemed like a wonderful place.

It was even more wonderful when she got home and found a note from Carol. "Party tomorrow on the beach (at the end of Surfrider Lane). Starts at noon!"

Kelly looked at Carol's round, regular handwriting and sighed. Great. Now was her chance to make up for that lousy Fourth of July party. She ran into her mother's office to ask if she could go.

"Is there a chaperone?" Mrs. Marshall asked, looking up from her bookkeeping work.

Kelly's heart sank. If Mom was going to start being overprotective, she'd just scream. She had never argued with her folks before, but if they thought they could keep treating her like a child . . . .

She broke off the thought and tried to keep her voice calm. "I don't know, but it's just a bunch of kids meeting on the beach. . . . I'll be home before night."

Mrs. Marshall thought a moment, and then smiled.

"I suppose, then, as long as it's daytime."

Kelly hugged her mother and ran up to her own room. She picked out her favorite bathing suit. Luckily, it had side laces, so it would more or less fit her skinnier frame.

It seemed years before she finally put on the suit—with an extra-long T-shirt over it—and headed to the beach.

Gulls screeched overhead, like they were straining to be heard above the pounding surf. Kelly ran across the sand to where a group of kids sat around a barbecue pit. She saw all the food laid out on a blanket around the fire.

"Oh, was I supposed to bring something?" she asked, wishing she'd lost more than eight pounds and that she didn't feel so dumb.

"No," came a familiar voice. "Brian's folks treated."

Kelly nodded to Carol, who sat with Brian Greer. He had his arm around her. Figures, Kelly thought, and hated herself for being jealous. Anyway, neither Brian nor Carol looked comfortable sitting like that. They looked like a couple of little kids playing grown-up. At least Carol did; even in her two-piece suit which showed off her blooming figure.

Kelly spread her beach towel and flopped onto the warm sand. Somebody turned on a transistor radio. Somebody else yelled for food.

It felt good to be with people her own age. She didn't have to wipe noses or break up fights or worry about anybody. She could just have fun.

Except she didn't have fun. As usual, she sat alone. She didn't dance or play volleyball because nobody asked her to. She didn't eat because it would break her diet. It was beginning to look like all she would do was sit and watch herself sunburn.

Then Brian Greer, as the resident "older man" decided to teach everybody how to surf—at least, all the girls. Kelly had no intentions of trying to do it—the very idea scared her to death. But at least it would be fun to watch. That, she decided, was the story of her life; always watching while other kids had fun. Dumb! Absolutely dumb! A person who was almost fourteen should be *doing* things, not watching others do them.

Kelly sighed and went back to watching. Several kids had brought boards. People took turns going out, always with Brian playing the teacher. Kelly wondered if he stayed so busy because he wasn't sure how to act around Carol. Maybe. Carol looked a little relieved. She seemed more comfortable cheering the surfers than she had sitting with Brian.

She didn't look so comfortable when Brian came running from the water, spewing sand and sea-drops all around him.

"Come on, girl. It's your turn," he said, and grabbed a board for her. Kelly almost giggled. Carol wasn't a good swimmer, and she'd never admit that to Brian. She'd be scared. But she'd go. It served her right. Kelly caught her eye, giving her an arched-eyebrow look that said so.

Carol wrinkled her nose and then turned to Brian. "Why don't we get Kelly to go, too?"

Kelly froze, as Brian noticed her.

"Come on. You haven't tried yet."

"Yeah, Kelly," somebody else said, "go on."

She was caught. She didn't want to look like a dud in front of everybody. But the very idea of skimming across the water on a cigar-shaped hunk of fiberglass scared her to death.

"Maybe I'll go later—now I want a hot dog," she said, throwing her diet to the winds in the face of this new threat.

"No, wait on the hotdog," Carol told her, and Brian just grinned.

It was no use. The whole thing made Kelly tremble with anger that she dared not show. Carol did this to her for one reason. She knew that she would look terrible out there—but Kelly would look worse.

Kelly took the board that someone held out to her and moved closer to Carol. "I'll get you for this," she muttered under her breath.

Carol just giggled and followed Brian to the water, with Kelly trudging behind.

In a flashing minute Kelly remembered that time in the sixth-grade Christmas play when she was a little crippled child at the manger and Carol was, predictably, the Virgin Mary. Carol had fluffed one of her two lines and everybody teased her about it afterwards.

"That was real dumb," they said.

Carol puckered her pretty face. "Don't call me dumb. Ask Kelly if you want to know about dumb. She's the one with the retarded sister."

Kelly could still remember the words. She remembered her pain. Most of the kids hadn't known about Becky then. But they had stopped teasing Carol to ask all of those wide-eyed hurting questions. Could people catch it like the measles? Did Becky go to the bathroom by herself? Did she drool and look weird and things like that? Kelly had run away crying. She had never really forgiven Carol for that.

Now here she was again; going to look like a fool because of Carol. She gritted her teeth and plunged into the water behind Brian. It was stinging cold, too. She slipped on seaweed and banged her foot on a rock.

"Paddle out on the boards," Brian called. He bellied down and made for an incoming wave. "Get on when I tell you—keep one foot in front of the other—don't panic—use your arms for balance." He screamed to be heard over the ocean's roar.

For Kelly, there was no Carol anymore, no Brian. There was only the raging ocean, a voice shouting fearful instructions, and a gull crying overhead.

"Now! Go for it!"

Kelly pushed her board into the wave. She felt the forward rush, sensed the surging break ahead.

"Stand up, stupid!"

She couldn't. The pulses in her temples threatened to blow out the sides of her head. Somewhere she heard Carol yell as she wiped out. Kelly could only hang on, pressing her whole body against the board that was now a victim of the pounding surf. She rode in to a burst of laughter, an awful defeat.

"That's the wildest style I've ever seen," Brian laughed, shaking the water from his hair as they dragged the boards ashore.

Kelly looked at him—the blond surfer god, so sure of himself. Carol, drenched and grinning, came to stand beside him, to join the laughter. Kelly wanted to cry and run away, the way she'd done in sixth grade. But she couldn't do that. She was almost fourteen, and that meant she had to handle it a new way.

"I invented it myself," she said, and forced a light-sounding laugh. "I promised the Hawaiians I'd go over and give 'em lessons."

It worked. It always did. The kids laughed. Kelly Marshall might not be a good surfer, but at least she was a good sport. Dumb kids! They probably thought that the salted drops on her cheeks were just left over from the ocean.

Chapter Seven

Kelly told Joel the awful story on the bus, between times of settling down kids who were excited about going to the carnival at the Tres Cerros Shopping Mall. She even told about what Carol had done in sixth grade.

"I hate her when she pulls things like that," she said.

Joel chomped on a candy bar he had brought along. "So how come you want a friend like that?"

Kelly had never really thought of that before. For one thing, she had always been so busy with Becky that she didn't have time to seek out friends. People had to come to her—and not many did. Besides, Carol wasn't the kind of girl you thought of *not* wanting for a friend. If she wanted you, you were her friend. That was it.

"I guess I'm jealous of her," Kelly said. "But I like her and all. Carol's smart and pretty and knows how to do everything."

"But she's a lousy person," Joel finished.

"That's a rotten thing to say!" Kelly was secretly glad that he had said it, though. "Look, she's my only real friend ... besides people who work with the kids, I mean."

"From what you told me, she's some friend." Joel, who had become almost as quick as Kelly in dealing with the kids, reached over the seat to make Michael let go of Lisa's hair. Then he settled back and shrugged. "You're weird. I mean, you see the good in these kids. You work with them and take up for them. But then you get all impressed by somebody like that Carol."

"Big philosopher! Are you just being mean for free, or are you worried about something?" Kelly just had to change the subject. Before Joel could answer, she reached across the aisle to pick up the stuffed rabbit that Billy Jackson had dropped.

"I'm not being mean at all, just trying to be a friend. But you're right, I am worried. I talked to Mrs. Riker last night. She's really down on those schools that wouldn't keep Marcy. Do you know why?"

Kelly nodded. "Yeah. They're the fancy kind—boarding schools. They don't like kids that cause trouble."

"But neither does Mrs. Riker," Joel hissed under his breath. "Why is she making such a big deal about Marcy? I mean, she said something about not liking to take kids whose parents aren't involved.

Kelly knew about Mrs. Riker's feelings on that subject. It was one of her big hang-ups. The director had all sorts of big ideals about what retarded kids could do, but she said they couldn't do it with just school. They needed help at home, too. Kelly avoided telling all that to Joel. It would just set him off on a big gripe against his parents.

"I think Mrs. Riker will take Marcy—if we can really do what we're trying to do."

"And if not, it's a state institution, this time. My folks have about figured out how to get by with that without looking bad in front of their fancy friends."

Kelly winced. She didn't know what to say. Fortunately, she didn't have to say anything. The bus got to the shopping center and the driver pulled up in sight of the cotton candy booth.

Of course, everybody wanted some of the pink fluff right away. Nobody could wait and nobody could keep quiet. It had to be *now*.

"Impatient, aren't they?" Joel grumbled, as he frantically passed cones into eager little hands.

Kelly was busy doing the same thing. "Yeah. Retarded kids have trouble learning to wait. Time is different for them, I guess."

Several kids just had to pinch the stuff, getting their fingers all sticky. Billy Jackson did worse than that. He sneezed just as he took the cone and caused an explosion of spun sugar. The next thing that exploded was Billy Jackson.

"Want more! More!" Billy shrieked. He wouldn't quit crying until Kelly handed him another one. Then the tears disappeared instantly.

"What did you do? Wave a magic wand?" Joel asked.

"Might say. That's one real plus retarded kids have. Most of them forget their hurts fast."

Becky and Marcy came dancing around, both pointing to the merry-go-round. "Taper music," Becky said, bouncing in time to the boom-da-boom of the sound.

"Ride pony," Marcy yelled, at almost the same moment.

Kelly held up her hands like a traffic cop. "Hold it! We can ride the ponies when we finish the cotton candy. But the taper isn't here."

Becky's lower lip jutted out. The usually sunny little girl could go into a huge sulk when she couldn't get something she wanted badly.

"Now don't start that," Kelly said, her voice firm but not snappish. "We're going to have fun today."

"But taper . . ."

"We'll practice with it at home."

Becky still looked disappointed as she finished her cotton candy, but not as pouty as before. Finally, she went with Marcy to the merry-go-round, and Kelly breathed a sigh of relief.

"Honestly, that kid. She'll let you forget her food, her toys—anything but that stupid tape recorder."

Joel fell in beside Kelly as they followed the girls to the merry-go-round. "I'm kind of glad she did that. I was beginning to think Becky was about perfect."

Kelly laughed and shook her head. "Not hardly. She's spoiled, I guess—sometimes."

"It's probably easy to spoil a cute kid like that, especially when she needs extra help."

"Cute kids always get spoiled. Even when they don't need extra help," Kelly muttered, and she wasn't thinking of Becky.

"Bitter, bitter," Joel teased.

Kelly didn't have time to answer. She was too busy helping Marcy and Becky onto wooden horses. The platform shivered a warning as she scooped Marcy into her arms and sat her down on a white horse with green polka dots. She cinched the safety belt and jumped to the ground, just as the music started.

Everybody rode once and then yelled to go around again. Kelly was trying to help Mrs. Riker pay the attendant and count heads. Just at that moment, Marcy decided that she wanted to find another horse.

Kelly yelled for Joel to undo her belt.

When she climbed down, she ran around the platform, faster than Joel could follow. Kelly cut across and found Marcy at the back of the platform, trying to pull Billy Jackson off his horse. Only the leather strip saved Billy from toppling to the ground before Kelly could grab Marcy.

"Want pony," the little girl yelled.

Kelly had to carry her off the platform.

"You can have another pony. That one's Billy's."

Marcy planted her thin legs wide apart. "Pony. Pony," she sobbed.

When the music started and the merry-go-round began its stately circle, Marcy wailed like someone had stabbed her. "Ranger! Ranger!"

Kelly stared at the child and then looked sharply at Billy Jackson's pony as it passed. She had to yell to be heard over Marcy's shrieks. "Look at Billy's horse."

Joel looked. The horse was brown, the mane and tail, light tan. "You mean she thinks that's really Ranger?"

"Maybe. Anyway, she doesn't realize that you treat *things* different from living . . . well, you know, people or animals."

"But even a retarded kid senses when something's alive . . ."

"Probably," Kelly cut in, while holding Marcy who was still yelling. "But that's not the point."

They stopped talking until they got Marcy calmed down. When she only whimpered softly to herself, Joel threw up his hands.

"So what is the point?"

"That she would hurt Billy—who's alive—to get the horse—which isn't."

"So what?"

"So we teach her the difference between live things and . . . well, unlive ones."

That afternoon, when all the merry-go-rounds and ferris wheels and bumper cars had been ridden, when the kids were safely home, Kelly took Joel shopping. They bought stuffed animals and one huge—and very real looking—doll. By the time they were through, they had made a weird Noah's Ark of pairs.

But Noah wouldn't have recognized the pairs; a live person and a toy doll, a hopping, twitching rabbit and a still, stuffed one. They had even found a stuffed toy pony that looked like a small Ranger.

Kelly liked Tatters toy twin best of all, with its brown curly coat and bright, button eyes.

"Don't forget," Kelly told Joel as she placed the toy dog and Tatters together in Marcy's lap, "we don't want to give her the idea that she can ruin things."

Joel snorted and shook his head until his blond hair made a pale wave across his forehead. "That's all we need . . . change one problem for another."

Kelly took Marcy's hand and told the little girl to pet Tatters. The puppy wagged his tail and licked her hand. "Alive . . . feels good," Kelly said.

She did the same thing with the stuffed dog. Marcy petted and smiled and cooed. No tail wagged. No trembling tongue licked her hand. "Not alive . . . can't feel good," Kelly said.

Tatters ran off to chase an offending fly. He jumped and nipped into the air and then sprawled in a belly-flop on the crabgrass.

Marcy laughed. She looked down at the stuffed dog on her lap and then back to Tatters. She blinked fast, several times. Her mouth opened, then closed, as if she had started to speak but then couldn't think of the words. Instead, she scrambled to her feet and ran after Tatters, leaving the toy dog lying in the damp grass.

"It's a good start," Kelly said, and grinned happily at Joel.

"I hope it works . . . and fast. There's not much summer left, you know. My folks are supposed to meet with Mrs. Riker just after show-and-tell night."

"And she'll decide then, about Marcy?"

"Yeah. And I'm scared. I don't think Mrs. Riker likes my folks."

Kelly didn't say anything. There was nothing to say. Knowing Mrs. Riker's ideas on parental involvement, she'd bet Joel was right. And that didn't make her feel very good at all.

Chapter Eight

Summer got down to business in August, with hot days without the usual ocean breezes to soften them. The whole world seemed like it was waiting for something.

Kelly felt the same way. Everything was about to happen; the end of the summer program, the verdict on Marcy, the freshman class election. This was the summer of contact lenses and diet foods, of kids and animals. Soon she would see how it would all turn out.

It looked good. At least she wouldn't go into high school as the chubby girl with glasses and a retarded sister. She'd be the almost-slim girl with contact lenses and a retarded sister. People always remembered Becky. There was never any getting away from it.

Kelly sighed and looked into the mirror of her white antiqued dresser. "Not bad, Kelly kid," she said. With nearly fifteen pounds of fat gone, she was even beginning to get what everybody called "a figure." Kelly wondered what it would be like to be a grown-up high school girl with a figure. Maybe she really would get elected to a class office.

Then maybe people would say, "You know Kelly, she's the one on student council."

It was a beautiful dream. But a scary one. Freshman orientation was only a couple of weeks away, and she'd hardly thought about the big speech she'd have to make.

"Kelly . . . Kelly . . . taper go."

Becky came charging into the room, gold curls flying. Kelly almost snapped something about knocking first, but she caught herself in time.

"You're not supposed to use that alone."

"Mama help."

"Good," Kelly said, and hugged the little girl to make up for her crossness. "When you learn how to use it, you can do it alone." She said that often because Becky liked to hear it.

The little girl giggled and bounced. She handed microphone to Kelly. "Talk!"

Kelly grinned. "My name is Kelly Marshall, and . . . and Becky is my little sister . . ." she kept on, saying whatever came to mind. Becky pushed the record button, standing straight-legged and proud as she taped her sister's words. When Kelly stopped talking, Becky pushed rewind and waited impatiently, tapping her fingers on the plastic case. She puckered her brow and pushed "play."

"You've done it," Kelly said, but Becky was staring at the machine like it was a disloyal friend. "No talk," she said, and her lower lip jutted out.

"Wait. You just went back a little far . . ."; the sound of her recorded voice cut in then and Becky chortled. She turned the machine off and held it close to her chest.

"Taper mine now," she said.

Kelly almost laughed. Becky sounded so important, so sure of herself. "Yes. It's yours now. I'm proud of you."

"Me, too," Becky said, and threw her arms around her sister's neck.

A mist covered Kelly's eyes. It was such a great feeling when one of the children learned something new. And you knew you'd helped. Kelly felt like telling the whole world what Becky had done. Call her friends. Put it in the paper. But nobody would care. What was the big deal about learning to work a simple cassette recorder? Kelly sighed. "I care," she whispered. "Thanks God."

"Come on," she said to Becky. "Let's tell everybody how good you've done. You can even use that for show and tell."

Becky and her recorder became the center of attention at the program. For a couple of days Becky Marshall was resident expert. Every child in the program came to her, asking to have some sound taped. There was a party at home, with a big cake to celebrate the great achievement. Then things went back to normal.

But it was a new kind of normal. In a small way Becky was a new kind of person. She had gained a skill. More importantly, she had gained new self-confidence.

Becky had always been a little ham. She liked nothing better than making people smile, being the center of attention.

The combination of the new skill with her "taper" and the upcoming show-and-tell gave her a big chance to do just that.

Kelly started early, coaching her for the big performance. "I learned to make this work by myself," she would say, and prove it by recording her own words.

"I wish Marcy's was as easy to figure," Joel said one morning, while listening to Becky practice. All the aides and teachers were busy thinking of something for each child to do. Most of the kids would say something about going to the zoo or the beach or the carnival. Kelly and Joel wanted something more special for Marcy. It had been an important summer in her life.

The angry little girl of June was almost gone in August. In her place was a child who could smile—at least sometimes. Marcy still got mad, and it would be a long time before she won any popularity contests. But at least she didn't look so pinched and nervous.

She was better—much better. Maybe Mrs. Riker would take her in spite of her parents. Kelly studied Marcy for a minute.

"What about the animals—playing with the animals?"

"Yeah," Joel said, quickly enthusiastic. "How about, 'I played with animals. They're fun.'"

Kelly's brown eyes flashed in her newly slim face. "Great! And she can show Tatters."

That settled it. Kelly and Joel got busy with morning rehersals and afternoon sessions for Marcy and the pairs. It was good and warm and friendly, working with Joel and the kids. It wasn't so good, working alone on her student council speech.

Kelly spent evenings in her room, trying to think of all the reasons why people should vote for her. The only one she could think of was that she wanted to be elected. She nibbled three pencil erasers to bits and, on the night before freshman orientation, was in a blind panic.

There was only one thing to do. She called Carol. "I can't think of a speech. How's yours coming?"

"I've had it done for days," Carol said, with a satisfied little giggle.

That figured, Kelly thought, but she forced down her jealousy. "Got any ideas for me?" For the first time ever, it bothered her to go to Carol, asking favors. She kept thinking about what Joel had said. She'd never questioned things with Carol before. She was her one, true friend. It was an honor to go around with her. It was that simple. At least, it used to be that simple. Now Kelly felt put down, having to turn to her for help.

Carol obviously enjoyed playing expert. "Tell how great you are, but sound modest. Tell how you want to help the council keep in touch with freshmen. Throw in something corny about how hard it is to be growing up, going into high school, and how we've all got to help each other."

Carol's ideas were so good that Kelly began to feel dumb for resenting her. Maybe she did think a lot of herself. Maybe she did like to lord it over Kelly. But why not? She was better at most things. And she *did* help whenever she was asked.

"That sounds great," Kelly said. "Are you saying anything about how hard it is, growing up?"

"Not me. But you're more down-to-earth. The kids know how you work at that retarded place—at least the kids from our school. And don't forget, we've got a big plus: Fremont is the biggest junior high in town, so we have more chances for votes."

Kelly hardly heard the last part. She was too busy wincing over "down-to-earth" and "that retarded place." But she didn't say anything. After all, Carol was trying to help. Kelly was used to some of the dumb things she said, without thinking.

"Listen, thanks for the ideas. You scared about tomorrow?"

She was sure that Carol would say no. But the voice on the other end trembled a little. "I guess so . . . all those people. But I'll be okay."

"Sure you will." It made Kelly feel good to be comforting Carol for a change. She felt warmer toward Carol right away. "Good luck tomorrow," she said.

"Thanks. Hope the ideas help."

"They will."

And they did. Kelly stayed up until midnight, but she got her speech outlined and ready to go. It sounded good; all about how she would help freshmen whenever she could, about her dreams that all of them would enjoy their high school experience together.

That night, she dreamed of taking bows, of shaking hands and being the center of attention. It was a beautiful dream. But somehow it ended with everyone laughing at her—and then it wasn't beautiful anymore. Kelly woke up crying at five in the morning. She lay in bed, rehearsing her speech and watching the dawn come up over the mountains.

This had to work. It just had to. Kelly wondered, though, if she'd ever get through her speech. She had never been more scared in all her life. Her folks fussed because she couldn't eat breakfast, and she ended up stomping out of the kitchen in a huff.

"Now, Kelly, you settle down," her mom said.

Why couldn't she understand? This was the most important day of Kelly's life. Who cared about breakfast?

Becky followed her mother and sister out of the kitchen, ignoring her father's call to come back to the table. "I not hungry, too," she said.

"You see?" Mrs. Marshall said under her breath.

Blast Becky anyway—that was another problem with retarded kids. If they loved somebody, they just blindly followed what that somebody did.

At that moment, Kelly wished Becky had never been born. She wished she, herself, had a family like Carol's, who saw the importance of being popular and special.

"All right! All right," she grumbled. There was no use fighting it. She went back to the table and ate eggs that had turned cold. Then she rushed out of the house. She rode her bike so wildly that a policeman gave her a dirty look just as she turned onto the campus of Tres Cerros High School.

The high school! Kelly felt more grown-up just walking onto the green, rolling grounds with the salmon-colored Spanish buildings. It seemed to be the wonderland where all her dreams would come true—if she could just get through one little speech.

She was glad that the assembly came first. The principal would talk, some of the upper classmen who had been elected to council last spring would talk. Then came the candidates.

Kelly tried to picture it all in her mind as she walked down the broad pathway that led to the auditorium. There was a big sign outside the front door: FRESHMEN ASSEMBLE AT NINE A.M. SHARP. CANDIDATES FOR CLASS OFFICE REPORT BACKSTAGE.

That's me, Kelly thought, pride coming through her fear. She went backstage and started to look for Carol. She forced herself to speak to John Simpson. He was from Cabrillo Junior High and—even though that was one of the smaller schools—he was probably going to be class president. Everybody in town knew John. His dad was a big lawyer, and he had gone around to all the five junior highs on the debating team. Kelly had never liked him. He seemed awfully impressed with himself. And he wasn't as good looking as Brian Greer, so he didn't have as much excuse to be stuck-up.

Kelly almost giggled to think of how Joel would feel about her opinion. He wouldn't like John, but then he'd think she was petty for putting so much emphasis on looks.

Come to think of it, she decided, that was kind of petty. But anyway, she hoped that being on the council wouldn't mean having to be too friendly to the John Simpsons on campus.

Kelly said good-bye to John and went on with her search for Carol. Onstage, she could hear the Principal begin the welcoming words to the new freshmen. Backstage, everybody looked nervous; even the older kids who were already on student council. Kelly recognized a redheaded girl named Marilyn Jennings. She had a kid brother at Becky's school. And she was secretary of the whole student council. Having a retarded kid in the family hadn't stopped her. It wouldn't stop Kelly, either.

Still, she wished she could find Carol. Right now, she could use a dose of her friend's confidence. She looked at all the groups of students, standing around talking and trying to pretend they weren't scared. No Carol. She looked in the dark corners of the backstage area, moving softly over the squeaking hardwood floors.

She found Carol just as the student council president began her talk. Her friend was in the narrow hallway that led to the dressing rooms. She leaned against a dirt-streaked white wall, right next to where somebody had scrawled, "Tres Cerro High . . . GO! GO! GO!"

One look told her that Carol wouldn't be giving out any doses of confidence today. She went over to the shaking girl.

"Are you okay?"

"I think I'm going to throw up. Oh, Kelly, I think I'm going to throw up . . . really."

Kelly put her arm around her friend. "It's a lousy time to get stomach flu."

"Not stomach flu! Fear! Sheer fear!" Carol pressed hard against her chest, taking quick, shallow breaths. "Quick! A restroom!"

Kelly scanned the area, thinking fast. There had to be a girls' room, but she couldn't see it.

"Hurry, Kelly, hurry!"

"Come on," Kelly said, remembering that she had seen one just down the back stairs. She began to run, fairly dragging Carol along with her. They plunged down the dark hallway, right into John Simpson, who looked at them like they were crazy and hurried on past.

Outside, Carol began to gasp and heave. Kelly pushed her into the girl's room and took her to a sink. Nothing happened, except for dry heaves.

"I want to throw up, but I can't," Carol moaned.

"Take it easy. Just take it easy."

Carol trembled and heaved and whimpered, but slowly settled down. "Oh, Kelly, what if I don't win? I'll die if I don't win."

Kelly hugged Carol the way she sometimes did Becky. "You'll win. Now come on. Wash your face and let's get back."

Carol splashed water on her face and cranked a piece of paper towel from a machine that was covered with scratched-in dirty words. She dried and took several deep breaths. "You really think I'll win?"

"Sure. You're a winner, Carol. You're always a winner." There was some bitterness in those words, but Kelly didn't show that in her voice.

"I don't know. I just don't know." Carol scrunched up her face and looked totally miserable. "I never got to know kids from the other junior highs . . ."

"But ours is the biggest, remember?"

Carol actually smiled a little. "Right. I guess you're right."

"Sure. You said it yourself." A question formed in Kelly's mind, and she couldn't hold back from asking it. "Carol . . . do you always get sick like this, before something important?"

Carol gave a short little laugh and leaned back against the sink. "Oh, yeah. All the time. Remember way back in first grade, when I was Little Red Riding Hood in the parent's day play?"

Kelly nodded. "Now that you mention it." She had forgotten about that one. It was just another in a long list of things she wanted that Carol got. "It happened then?"

"That was the first time. My mom and dad had made such a big deal over the thing—made me do my lines over and over. My mom once wanted me to be an actress, you know, and I guess it was a big thing to her. Anyway, I was late, remember?"

Kelly didn't remember, but she nodded anyway.

"That was because I threw up all over my red cape and mom had to wash it." Carol spread her hands in a gesture of helplessness. "I've learned not to eat before anything big."

"It's weird, you know," Kelly said, feeling just a little hurt. "I never knew. I'm supposed to be one of your best friends, and I never knew." It seemed to her that friends should know things like that about one another.

"Usually it's all over by the time I get someplace. Sometimes, I even stick my finger down my throat so I can get it over with."

"But, wow . . . I mean, if you had told me, maybe I could have helped."

"It's not the kind of thing you tell anybody . . . even your best friend."

Kelly felt better when Carol called her a "best friend." That was quite an honor, being Carol's very best friend. "Hey, we'd better get back."

Carol looked like she didn't want to go. She fumbled in her purse for a comb and straightened out her long blond hair. "Don't tell anybody, okay, Kelly?"

Kelly promised, and the two girls hurried backstage. The student council president was just announcing a boy named Mike Parker, "our final candidate for Freshman Class Advocate."

"Final candidate—oh no!" Kelly stood on the verge of tears. All the plans and dreams, down the drain.

"Don't worry. Follow me, I'll fix it up." Carol seemed the picture of pretty blond confidence again. Maybe that was because she had something on her mind besides herself, Kelly thought. She followed, obediently, trembling and still fighting back tears.

Carol walked right up to the Principal. "Sir? This is my friend Kelly. She . . ." Carol hesitated, and in that moment,

Kelly thought she would die on the spot. ". . . she was sick, and I guess she missed the call."

The Principal was a tall balding man with kind eyes. "Can't you talk for yourself?" he asked Kelly. His tone was gentle, but she was so busy reeling from what Carol had said that he might as well have yelled at her. Why did Carol have to lie and add to the humiliation? It wasn't fair, it just wasn't fair. Kelly couldn't hold back the tears anymore, and she couldn't answer through her own sobs.

"Now relax," the Principal said. He laid a hand on her shoulder. "Honestly, some of you kids just aren't ready for these things. All right. All right. Pull yourself together. You can go on next."

It took all of Kelly's strength to stop crying, to bring the dream to life again. She took deep breaths. She dried her eyes with the backs of her hands. When she felt almost human again, she turned to Carol. Her eyes flashed. "Why did you say that?" she hissed under her breath.

"I was trying to help. He might not have let you go on if he thought you'd just been with me."

Carol's voice didn't even sound convincing. "You're lying. You're just out-and-out lying."

"Now that's not fair! If that's the way you feel, maybe we shouldn't be friends anymore."

Kelly wanted to sock Carol, but she didn't. "Maybe we never really were," she said, in a deadly quiet voice.

Carol backed away like she had been hit for real. She had probably thought that the threat of withdrawing friendship would bring Kelly right into line. She was used to being the popular one, the wanted one. The idea that someone—especially old Klutzy Kelly, who always idolized her—would *not* want to be her friend was totally strange to her.

Neither girl said anymore. Kelly would have liked to tell Carol off, once and for all—tell her for all the years of being put down—but she didn't have time. The Principal had gone onstage and the council president was talking to the audience. "We had a mixup backstage. There is a fourth candidate for Advocate. Miss Kelly Marshall."

She'd show Carol, Kelly thought, as she walked onstage. She'd do a great speech in spite of everything. Her footsteps sounded hollow and unbelievably loud as she made her way to the podium. Her knees shook so badly that, any minute, she

expected to hear giggles from the audience. She stubbed her toe as she stepped onto the platform. Her mind, stubborn and terrified, flashed, *I played with animals this summer. They're fun.* Her voice said, "I'm Kelly Marshall from Fremont Junior High, and I'd like to be Freshman Class Advocate. I feel I have something to bring to the position . . ."

Her voice steadied and sounded like it belonged to someone else; not to Kelly, who trembled and felt like crying. But the voice was softly saying things that she hadn't put into the carefully practiced outline.

". . . Because of my little sister, who's pure sunshine and lots of fun, but who's mentally retarded because my mom had measles while she was pregnant, I've grown used to working with people. I'm a teenaide at the school where Becky goes, and I've learned a lot from dealing with other staff members. I've learned how to organize, how to present ideas, how to understand other people's problems. Now, we're all lucky here. We're growing up normal. But we're growing up. And that means we're going to have lots of problems. Some of those problems will be about school, and some of them might be solved by the student council. I want to help. I want to listen to each of you, to make the freshman class officers aware of who needs what, and to help get those things when it's possible. Thank you for listening. I hope you'll vote for me."

Kids in the audience applauded loudly. A couple of them actually cheered. When Kelly got offstage, the principal shook her hand and said he was glad he'd let her go on. Kelly felt alive and free and happy. She was going to win. She could feel it in her bones. And she'd done it by being herself—not a faked copy of Carol. Just Kelly, talking about the things she knew.

She sat on an old bench backstage and tried to listen to the other speeches. A couple of people came by to congratulate her on a good speech. Someone said she had guts, talking about a retarded sister.

Guts? Maybe. But everybody at Fremont, at least, knew about Becky. She didn't have anything to lose. Kelly stopped her thoughts long enough to listen closely when Carol was called to the stage.

Of course she did great. She walked onto that huge, lighted stage, smiling like she'd never had a care in the world.

That was the Carol that Kelly had known all these years. Sure of herself. Always in control. And she paid such a high price for it. Nobody would suspect. Just like nobody would suspect how many times old klutzy Kelly had dreamed of being a movie star or a rock singer or maybe an Olympic figure skater.

Kelly grinned to herself. Maybe she wasn't pretty and graceful like Carol. But then she wasn't the one who got sick, either. No matter how much Carol lied, nothing could change the facts. And Kelly knew the facts. For the first time in a long time she *felt* like a winner.

Now there was nothing to do but wait for the voting.

Chapter Nine

The voting was over. So was the campus tour and the "club faire" in the quad. Kelly had liked that. The place had looked like a carnival—tables and signs and banners everywhere. Every club on campus had set up to tell all the incoming freshmen about their activities. Kelly had entertained herself by looking at the people surrounding the various tables.

She decided that she could tell what club was what, without even looking at signs. Bright, pretty girls with California tans and figures already blossomed jostled each other to find out about the Ebelles Social Club and the Pep Squad. Tall, well-built boys headed for the athletic programs. Radical looking types in peasant shirts and beads sought out political and service groups and the quiet, intelligent ones gathered around the science club exhibits.

Kelly had thought of Joel when she'd seen the Chemistry Club sign. She wrinkled her nose and wished he was there. He could have come. Orientation was for incoming upperclassmen, too. But Joel didn't care about things like that. And she'd been too proud to tell him the truth. "I want you there because I need you there." That sounded dumb. But he *was* her only real friend. She knew that now after this morning with Carol.

Friend or not, he probably would have bawled her out for being so shook up over the elections. But she was shook up.

And now it was time. The freshmen had reassembled in the auditorium for the announcement of class officers. Kelly sat in the front row with the other candidates, fidgeting in her seat. She had purposely gotten far away from Carol. She sat alone and dreamed. In her mind, she saw the Principal onstage, saw people applaud as he called Kelly Marshall for Class Advocate and somebody else—anybody but Carol—for secretary.

Carol would be crying; tears of defeat that she couldn't hide from anybody. No lies would protect her precious image. And Klutzy Kelly—all skinny and contact-lensed and smiling—would run up onstage to take a bow. "Fellow students, thank you for this honor. I will do my best in the coming year to be worthy of it."

Only it didn't happen that way. When it came time for class advocate, Kelly actually started to get up.

"Class advocate is Mike Parker."

It took a while for her to realize that the name she heard in the auditorium wasn't the one she'd heard in her dreams. She crumpled in her seat. To add insult to injury, she had to sit there, blinking back tears, while Carol accepted the office of class secretary.

It wasn't fair. It just wasn't fair. Kelly stared straight ahead, seeing nothing but blurr. Her teeth clamped sharply down on the soft flesh inside her cheeks. She couldn't cry. She wouldn't.

She didn't cry. At least not then. But when she finally got home to the safety of her room, heavy sobs rose from the pit of her stomach, wracking her whole body.

"Dreams just don't come true. They don't."

She stretched out on her bed and closed her eyes. She couldn't dream anymore. The dreams were dead. She didn't see a popular and successful Kelly. She saw another one—one she would rather forget.

This Kelly was dressed in yellow organdie, flocked with white roses. The puff sleeves and full skirt she'd wanted so badly only made her look fatter.

She was in fifth grade and it was Mayday.

She had made her construction paper baskets and filled them with flowers. She had even practiced the Maypole dance. Now she waited in the front school yard. She didn't sit down because she feared grass stains on her pretty new dress. Her gaze was glued to the porch of the main building. Mr. Mackie, the principal, stood beside an old chair that, with crepe paper and fresh flowers, had become an elegant throne. He held a crown in his hand. It was only gold foil paper, wrapped over a cardboard form. But it was the most beautiful thing Kelly had ever seen.

In a moment, perhaps she would wear it. She would sit on that throne, hear the music start, and stride regally down to

lead the Maypole dance. The pole was there, with a huge pink rosette at the very top. Streamers hung from it, floating on the spring breeze like fairy dresses. She would take the Queen's golden streamer, nod to the other children, and then dance in and out, around and around, until she and her court of dancing maidens had woven the delicate streamers together in a huge, upside-down May basket.

Mr. Mackie stepped forward and raised his hand for silence. "Boys and girls. Moms and dads. I have the honor of crowning our Mayday Queen. The students have chosen . . ."

Kelly Marshall. Kelly Marshall. Kelly Marshall! she prayed.

"Carol Maguire."

Kelly almost cried again, remembering how she had felt watching Carol lead the Maypole dance with that golden crown on her head.

She more-or-less heard people talking downstairs, then footsteps coming up the hallway.

"Hey, Kelly—it's me—Joel."

He sounded kind of sheepish and sad. Kelly tried to stop the tears, but her very effort made new ones. "Come on in."

Joel came in and stood in the doorway. He looked paler than usual. He laced his stained fingers together and stammered. "I . . . I called before. Your mom told me. I'm sorry . . ."

"It's the story of my life," Kelly burst out, and then angry words tumbled out of her. She told about the election, about Carol saying that she, Kelly, had been sick. She even told about the Mayday queen.

"That's really rotten. I mean, that Carol must be like my mother was, when she was young. Kelly, people like that . . . well, you just have to ignore them."

"Yeah," Kelly said softly. She wished that Joel would go away and leave her to her misery. She wanted to dig a hole inside herself and then just fold up into it until she vanished from the world. But even through her tears, she saw the concern, the understanding, on Joel's face. "I think you're my only real friend," she said.

Joel did just what she had known he would do. He blushed. Kelly smiled just a little, in spite of the pain inside. "Hey, if my folks will let us go out this late . . . how about having a pizza? My treat."

"Sounds great. But my treat. We're celebrating."

"Celebrating?"

"Sure!" Joel grinned, but his eyes still looked sad. "We're celebrating that you're not like Carol."

Kelly smiled. Maybe that was something to celebrate after all. But dead dreams were no cause for celebration. And she hurt inside. That was nothing to celebrate. She started to cry again, quieter this time. "Joel . . . do . . . do you think it's because . . . well, you know in my speech, I talked about Becky and all."

Joel looked like a trapped animal. "Maybe, Kelly . . ." he said, and the words obviously didn't come easily. "I know how kids feel about things; believe me, I've gotten flack because of Marcy. But if that's it, then it's still not you. I mean, maybe kids our age think the wrong things are important. They just don't understand, I guess."

"I guess not," Kelly said. For a moment, she hated Becky for existing, for being retarded. Then she hated the other kids for being so shallow. Last of all, she hated herself for all those feelings churning inside her. "Let's get that pizza," she said, and the words came out angry.

The phone rang just as the two of them started downstairs. "I'll get it," Kelly yelled, and took it in the upstairs hallway.

It was Carol. Kelly almost hung up on her. But the girl she had called friend for so long sounded near tears.

"I didn't mean what I said about us not being friends. I don't like it when people don't like me. Will you still be my friend, Kelly?"

All sorts of things flashed through Kelly's mind. Maybe she had been the strong one all along. Maybe Carol needed a klutz to make her feel good. "I don't hate you or anything. But we'll be doing different things now that we're in high school."

"I guess. Kelly? I'm scared. Do you think I'll be a good secretary?"

Kelly remembered how often Carol had asked those kind of questions. Funny she had never noticed before. Carol always needed people telling her how great she was. "You'll do fine," Kelly said. "Now I've got to go. A friend and I are going for pizza." She couldn't resist adding that last, letting Carol know that she finally had a life of her own.

Joel had listened quietly to the whole conversation. He

75

shrugged when Kelly hung up. Kelly shrugged back at him. "She wanted to know that I was still her friend . . . can't stand having people not like her, she said."

"Figures. Maybe that's the price people like that have to pay."

"Maybe."

The two friends smiled at each other and went downstairs.

Chapter Ten

On the day of the show-and-tell party, nothing seemed to go right. For one thing, it rained—or rather, drizzled and looked as gray as Kelly's mood. Becky got so excited that she wet her pants—something that she hadn't done in nearly two years. Marcy was walking around like a zombie, cuddling Tatters close to her and muttering to herself. Worst of all, the Simms' had a "social engagement" and didn't come.

"They're dumb, you know," Joel told Kelly, as they made their way past the folding metal chairs that had been set up in the multipurpose room. "How could they not come? They know how Mrs. Riker feel about parental involvement." Joel was so busy complaining that he ran into the curtain that had been put up to serve as a "backstage" for the young performers.

Kelly slipped through the curtain, stopping to wave to her folks, who already sat in the audience with a few other early arrivals. "They will make the interview, won't they?"

"Yeah," Joel mumbled. "They set it up for after the party. Made a big deal about how they would cut their plans short to be there. I know that really impressed Mrs. Riker."

Kelly winced. She could just hear the director griping about parents who tried to leave it all to the school. "Mrs. Riker does know how far Marcy's come this summer, though," she said, trying to be as encouraging as she could.

"I hope so. Kelly, you know, I don't think I could handle the guilt if that kid ends up in a state institution; and my folks are ready to hide her away there, believe me. They haven't even told their fancy friends in this town about Marcy—they could just pretend she doesn't exist."

Kelly squeezed Joel's arm. "You're really great to worry so much."

"Nope. Not really. I feel guilty, remember?"

Kelly remembered. And she figured he would never forget—not really. He was a sensitive boy. He'd always think, just a little, that if maybe he'd watched Marcy closer on that awful day—Kelly broke off the thought with a sigh. It didn't seem fair that people should have guilt trips all their lives for something that wasn't really their fault in the first place. But then, being almost fourteen, she was learning that a lot of things often didn't seem fair.

She didn't have much time to think about this point. She

told herself that God must have an answer somewhere and then got busy with the kids. She found lost show-and-tell objects, talked Joel into taking Tatters for a walk so he wouldn't embarrass them all, tied shoelaces and wiped noses. Especially wiped noses. Everybody seemed to have one of those late summer colds.

In all the confusion she heard Billy Jackson squeal. It was a happy sound, but sharp enough to draw her attention. What she saw scared her. Marcy and Billy were playing a strange game. They took turns touching each other's noses, stroking arms, and trying to count fingers. Of course, neither one of them could get to ten. It was all very sweet and gentle—except for the strange look on Marcy's face. The frail little girl was glassy-eyed, like she was seeing and feeling things that nobody else could know.

Kelly told herself that it was probably just stage fright. But she had horrible pictures of Marcy hurting someone or throwing a tantrum or otherwise wrecking her chances for fall.

Mrs. Riker's voice sounded over a rasping microphone, greeting the guests. "It's good for our children to look back and remember pleasant things. That's what we are going to share with you tonight."

She stepped off the raised platform that served as a stage, cramming her ample body past a crush of excited children.

Billy Jackson walked onstage, carrying the potted plant that was his show-and-tell. The little boy with the broad face and strangely shaped eyes grinned out at the audience. "I growed this from seeds," he said, chewing every word like it was a wad of gum.

People applauded loudly. Billy giggled and ran offstage. He looked like he might let out with a Tarzan yell at any moment. "I did. I did." He said.

Kelly gave silent applause of her own to Billy and then to each child who followed. Some stumbled over their words. Some just stood and stared, forgetting everything but to hold the objects they had brought. A couple of children started crying and ran back to the safety of the curtained area.

It didn't matter. They all tried. That was the important thing. When Becky's turn came, Kelly got an extra lump in her throat. She watched, as usual, from behind the curtain. But her heart was onstage with her little sister. She said her line perfectly. Then she played back a couple of minutes of the show which she had been taping.

She smiled when she walked offstage, but there was none of Billy's wild excitement in her. She moved with a slow and grand pride, like a princess.

Kelly and Joel both hugged her. Then Joel sucked a deep breath through his teeth. He didn't say anything. He didn't have to. It was Marcy's turn.

He handed Tatters back to Marcy. She turned without a word and walked slowly through the curtain. She stood squarely in front of the audience, head held high, feet planted wide apart. She wrinkled her nose and bounced Tatters gently in her arms.

"I played with animals," she began, firing out the words quickly. Kelly grabbed Joel's hand and grinned. It was going to be all right.

Then Marcy stopped.

She raised Tatters higher, so that his shaggy little face was close to her own. He licked her cheek.

She looked first to one side of the stage and then to the other. Her lips puckered into a pinched "O." Her eyebrows became jagged lines over her widening eyes.

"She's forgotten," Joel whispered.

"That doesn't matter."

It hadn't mattered with the other kids. But Marcy was different. Forgetting might make her blow. Kelly didn't want to say that to Joel. "They're fun. They're fun," she prompted. She cupped her mouth, trying to project the missing words to Marcy.

The little girl gave no sign of hearing. She looked down at Tatters with the same glazed expression that Kelly had seen backstage.

"Something awful's going to happen," Joel hissed.

He started to go onstage, but Kelly held him back. "Give her a chance."

The audience sensed Marcy's tension. They scuffled and coughed and rattled—all the things that people do when they are uncomfortable for someone on stage.

Marcy didn't notice. She was too busy looking at Tatters in that strange way. At last she looked out to the audience again. A slow smile began to spread across her lips. Her whole face glowed in a most un-Marcy-like fashion.

"They're . . . alive," she said, at first softly, then with a voice ringing confidence, "They're alive!"

The applause was bigger than ever before. People seemed to sense that something wonderful had just happened.

"She understands. Marcy knows," Kelly whispered, and the words lifted her like wings. She had known satisfaction before, working with the kids; like when Becky learned the recorder. But this was bigger. This was knowing that a child had at long last learned something important about life itself.

Joel hugged Kelly and, for once, didn't even blush. When Marcy scampered off stage, both of them grabbed her. Joel's voice came out in a gasp that was just this side of happy tears.

"You did great . . . just great."

"Don't squish Tatters," Marcy said, rescuing the puppy from the crunch of too many hugs. She grinned with her proud young teachers and then hurried away to be with some of the other children.

"You found the key," Joel said softly. There were tears in his eyes.

"*We* found it . . . all of us together. Marcy will make it now. Mrs. Riker won't turn her down no matter what your folks do. She'll make it."

"And so will you. It *is* a talent, you know," Joel said gently.

Kelly thought of Maypoles and elections, of glamor and popularity. She sighed.

"Maybe. Maybe it is."

They both laughed. Kelly felt warm all over. This summer, a retarded child had learned about life and love. She, old klutzy Kelly, had helped. And she could have done it fat, with glasses, just as well as skinny, with contacts. Maybe that did make her special in a quiet sort of way. Not glamorous. Not exciting. Not even Mayday Queen.

She grinned at the boy who had become her close and trusted friend. He looked happier, like maybe the guilt wouldn't sit so heavy anymore. He still didn't know the answers, but his question had changed. Instead of God why—he was asking God, how.

He grinned back and easily took her hand into his. Perhaps being almost fourteen wasn't so bad after all, Kelly thought. She smiled to herself, thinking that Marcy had taught them as much as they had taught her.